Praise for Avery Flynn's Books:

"Sexy and sassy... Avery Flynn brings it all."—*Carly Phillips, NY Times Bestselling Author*

"This book is so good you won't want to put it down."—*Harlequin Junkie, Enemies on Tap*

"Flynn intertwines fashionistas and fighters in book two of this heavily talked-about series and she'll leave readers breathless by the time they reach the heart-pounding finish."—*4.5 starts Top Pick, RT Book Reviews, This Year's Black*

Flynn knows her sass and sex ... sheer naughty fun!"—*Into the Fire author Amanda Usen, Betting the Billionaire*

"I loved this story."—*Darynda Jones, NY Times Bestselling Author, Jax and the Beanstalk Zombies*

"...Thrilling, funny passionate and even contains a few tips to keep the fashion police away from your doorstep."—*RT Book Reviews, High-Heeled Wonder*

Trouble on Tap

by

Avery Flynn

This book is a work of fiction. Names, characters, places, and incidents are the product of the author's imagination or are used fictitiously. Any resemblance to actual events, locales, or persons, living or dead, is coincidental.

Visit Avery's website at www.averyflynn.com.

Edited by KC

Cover design by Avery Flynn

Formatting by Anessa Books

ISBN 978-0-9908335-9-8 (digital)

ISBN 978-0-9964763-0-0 (print)

Manufactured in the United States of America

First Edition July 2015

To everyone who manages to fight another day even when things look FUBAR because they believe it will get better. And it will.

Chapter One

Three Years Ago

That all too familiar pre-deployment rush had kicked in a day and a half ago and Mateo Garcia was more than ready to get elbows-deep in the shit, but first he had to see *her*.

He glanced back up at the big-screen TV at the end of the bar, the one playing a fashion show where Olivia Sweet was owning the runway. Normally, the biggest game of the night or a mixed martial arts fight would be on; this *was* a Marine bar after all. But the owner obviously knew his target audience, and it had been a stroke of genius to turn on a pre-recorded lingerie fashion show instead of two teams battling it out for last place in the standings.

Every man in the room was salivating as Olivia strutted across the televised runway, her many assets on full display. She wore some sort of sparkly bra and panty set that was probably worth a cool million but the guys watching couldn't have cared less. She was a Recon Marine's wet dream brought to life—all curves and mile-long legs and a face so beautiful that it knocked every thought clear out of a man's head.

"There is no way you know her." Chance Ferrante sipped his beer. "No fucking way."

Not only did Mateo know her, he was going to be buried balls-deep inside her before the night was through. It was his and Olivia's secret pre-deployment tradition. They both got lucky with a no-strings fuck, and he and his team always made it home in one piece. "Care to bet on it?"

Chance's eyes lit up. His mama had named him appropriately because the man alway took a chance. "Name the terms."

Mateo almost felt guilty for hustling his friend this way. Then he remembered the vibrator TSA had found in his carry-on six months ago, and the howls of laughter from the rest of the team as they filed by through security. "Loser covers the team's bar tab."

The other man's eyes widened. "On the last night on the town before training lockdown?"

"Not a big deal, unless you think you're going to lose," Mateo said.

"Fuck you. You're on."

They clinked shot glasses and tossed back the tequila like water.

"So where's your proof?" Ferrante asked.

"You'll see soon enough." Mateo glanced at his watch. Only twenty minutes late. For Olivia, that was practically early.

"You are so full of shit, Garcia. With that pretty-boy face of yours, you pull in more tail on a daily basis than any other guy on the team but not even *you* are bringing in someone like Olivia Sweet."

There was movement by the bar's door and excited chatter zipped through the crowd.

A buzz of anticipation started at the base of his spine. His good-luck charm had arrived. Oh, the people in their small hometown would have a good laugh about that. Everyone in Salvation, Virginia, knew the Sweets were nothing but trouble, every crazy one of them. Not that it mattered to him what the gossips said; it wasn't as if he was ever going to end up back there again.

He finished his beer in one long pull. "Get out your wallet, Ferrante."

The bar patrons parted like the Red Sea as Olivia did her sexy walk across the room. She didn't miss a step as she strutted toward him. Beautiful and Amazon-tall in spiked high heels, she wore a short red trench-coat dress that was unbuttoned at the top, giving the illusion that her tits were about to spill out. On some people it would have looked bulky, but on her tall, hourglass, supermodel body, it was enough to make his tongue stick to the roof of his mouth. Especially since he knew exactly what was under it—not a damn thing but her luscious body.

She stopped in front of him. "Buy a girl a drink?"

"I know Ferrante here would be happy to get your drink, along with covering everyone else's tab."

The other Marine shook his head in amazement and reached for the wallet in his back pocket.

Mateo got up off his bar stool and held it out for her. She sat down and tossed her hair over one shoulder. The position gave him the perfect angle to look down the deep-V neckline of her dress. His cock twitched at the sight.

This was their game. They played it every few months, whenever one of them could hop a plane and sneak away for a weekend of hot sex. She met him somewhere public wearing the absolute minimum amount of clothing. He'd hold out as long as he could until he had to drag her to his hotel room, where they'd fuck until they were both too exhausted to do anything but breathe.

If he'd been a better kind of man, he'd worry about falling for Olivia Sweet, but the truth was that he wasn't. He wasn't a man made for commitments—watching the ugly implosion of his parents' marriage had turned him off that institution for good. But a good time? Oh he was ready for that any time, any place—which is what made his arrangement with the wild child of Salvation so perfect.

Olivia looked up at him as she toyed with the thin gold chain around her neck that disappeared between the deep valley of her tits. "Like the view?"

"It's unbelievable." And it was. He wasn't going to last long before he had to touch her.

Tomorrow morning, he and his team were headed out to train at a place they couldn't even tell their families about. To everyone outside of a select number who qualified as need-to-knows, their second tour in Afghanistan would just be business as usual, when in reality it was anything but. He had less than twelve hours before training lockdown and he wasn't about to waste it in a bar when Olivia was here.

The elevator doors had barely shut before Olivia's fingers were at the buckle of the belt cinching the waist of her trench dress. Drunk on his nearness, she ignored the security camera in the ceiling. It didn't mean a damn thing. Hell, who was she kidding? She was the wild Sweet triplet, the one voted most likely to do anything, and all she wanted to do right now was Mateo.

"Take it off." His hungry gaze never left her as he inserted the penthouse keycard into the slot above the floor buttons.

The elevator jerked ever so slightly as it rose at a glacial pace and she adjusted her stance to better balance on her four-inch heels. The last thing she wanted was to tumble onto her ass during a striptease. Not tonight. Not with Mateo. She'd spent most of her life half in love with him. Making a fool of herself in front of him wasn't an option.

"The penthouse? Really?" She untied the belt around her waist. The material loosened around her, the sudden influx of air sweeping against her overheated skin.

"I'm a man without commitments or a permanent address unless it's attached to a military base. What else am I going to blow my money on other than outrageously expensive hotel rooms to fuck you in until you forget your name?" His green-hazel eyes had turned dark with barely reined-in lust. "Now, stop teasing."

She inched down the zipper. Slowly. She loved pushing him like this. He'd snap. He always did. And the explosion would be so worth it—for both of them.

He leaned back against the closed elevator doors and crossed his arms, the move making his biceps bulge. "I said take it off."

She toyed with the zipper but didn't lower it even a millimeter more. Her nipples puckered against the dress's soft leather, warmed by her desire-heated skin. "Here? In the elevator?"

Something dangerous flashed in his eyes. Hard. Wild. Ravenous. "Yes."

She clenched her core muscles tight. She couldn't help herself, teasing him turned her on. "Why should I?"

"Because you want to." He closed the distance between them in one swift step, crowding her up against the back of the elevator, centering himself between her open legs. "You want to show the security guard watching the video feed and jerking off behind his desk just how hard your perfect pink nipples are and how slick your sweet pussy is just from thinking about me touching you, licking you, fucking you senseless. You're so turned-on you're going to ruin that leather dress you're barely wearing if you're not careful."

Heart hammering in her chest, she realized she'd pushed him right up to the edge where rigid control gave way to ferocious hunger. All it would take was the smallest verbal tap to tip him right over. "I'm not wet."

"Prove it." He pressed his hands to the wall on either side of her shoulders and dipped his head so that his hot breath caressed the sensitive skin of her earlobe. "Touch yourself right now."

Refusing wasn't an option. Not when she ached for this—for him. His touch. His body. His mouth. She slid her fingers down the rough metal line of the half-closed zipper to the dress's short hem. Watching him through her eyelashes as he watched her, she drew out her actions, pulling the tension higher.

"You know what happens when you make me wait," he growled.

She did. And she loved it. But she'd skated the edge for too long, ever since she'd slid across the backseat of the limo, her bare ass on the leather reminding her of exactly who she was going to see and what she was going to do.

Biting her bottom lip, she slipped her hand under her dress and glided her fingers across her plump wet folds.

"Show me." A strained hoarseness tightened his tone.

Unable and unwilling to deny him, she withdrew her hand from under her dress and held it up between them. There was no missing the moisture glistening on her fuck-me-red nails.

"You should know you can't lie to me." He grabbed her wrist and raised her hand to his mouth, taking her fingers inside and sucking off her juices with just enough pressure to make her glad there was a wall behind her to hold her up. "Now, take off the damn dress."

No slow tease now. She couldn't take it any longer. Just a swift downward jerk on the zipper pull and the dress parted. The cool air swept across her bare flesh as she shrugged the leather off her shoulders. It fell to the elevator floor. Heat licked her skin as his heady gaze traveled across her exposed body.

A *bing* sounded.

The elevator doors whooshed open.

Olivia's heart blocked her throat and she slapped one arm across her breasts and dropped the other so her hand blocked a direct view of her pussy.

Mateo chuckled.

That's when she took a good look at the scene beyond his broad shoulders. Marble floors. A leather couch. Wall-to-ceiling windows showing the city's skyscraper-dotted skyline. It had been a private elevator leading directly to his penthouse suite and he'd obviously known it the whole time.

"Bastard." She leaned down and swiped her dress off the elevator floor before swerving around him and strutting her way into the room, stopping only when she stood facing the windows—all the better to watch his approach in the reflection.

"What?" He followed her into the room, depositing his cufflinks in a small bowl by the now-closed elevator doors. "Thinking you were going to walk naked down the hallway didn't make that sweet pussy of yours even softer and wetter for me?" He made fast work of the buttons on his crisp white shirt as he prowled across the room, stripping as he went. "You forget; I know you. I know everything about you. I know what turns you on. What makes you melt. What makes you keep coming back for more."

He stopped halfway to her, his hands on the top button of his pants. Naked from the waist up, he was fucking perfection. Broad shoulders. Muscles that rippled with his every move. A knowing smirk that got her wet faster than the rest of the package because he was right. He did know her—the good, the bad and the Sweet.

She turned around and walked over to him with enough of a runway stomp to make her breasts jiggle. Pushing away his hands, she unfastened his pants then let her touch linger on his closed zipper. "And the security guard watching the feed?"

"Oh, I paid him very well to ignore that particular monitor tonight." He brushed the back of his knuckles across her puckered nipple before pinching it between his thumb and first finger and pulling it taut. "The time for playing with zippers is over, Olivia."

A smartass retort died on her lips when he grabbed her hips and tossed her over his shoulder. Her cheek landed against the sinewy planes of his back. She smoothed her palms against his muscle as he strode out of the living room and into the bedroom. He kept her like that, with her hips across his shoulder and her bare ass in the air, as he flipped off his shoes. His pants were next.

"Just look at that." He rubbed circles across her butt.

Bracing her hands against his back, she lifted herself and twisted enough to look over his shoulder. He'd stopped in front of a full-length mirror. He was watching her, and she couldn't look away from him as her gaze traveled up from his thick, corded thighs to the hard cock jutting from their juncture. He looked good enough to make a girl pray for mercy.

"I could stare at your ass all night." He smacked it lightly, the delicious sting spreading from her cheeks to her clit.

"That seems like a waste of the evening," she said, her breathy tone giving away exactly how beyond teasing she was.

He pivoted away from the mirror and flung her onto the king-size bed. Her landing was as soft as he was hard. His hands glided up the outside of her thighs with a firm pressure as his lips, maddeningly soft, traveled up the inside of her left leg. The higher he reached, the less she could think. All she could do was feel the rasp of his five o'clock shadow on her calf, the sharp sting of his teeth as he nipped the soft flesh above her knee, and the pressure of his thumbs as he gripped high on her thighs and pushed her legs wide.

"My good-luck charm is so wet for me." He circled her opening with a finger before plunging it inside. "After how you made me wait in the elevator, I should tease you until you beg for my cock."

She lifted her hips off the bed, taking his finger in deeper. It was good, but not enough. What she craved was thicker, longer and more filling than his finger. "Please."

He added a second finger. "Tell me what you want."

"You." She dropped back to the bed and reached out to the bedside table. They'd done this in enough hotel rooms that she knew exactly where to find what she was looking for. "Inside me." She yanked open the drawer, reached inside, pulled out a condom and threw it at him. "Now."

He reached up one large hand and snagged it out of the air as it flew overhead. "Impatient, aren't you?"

Watching him roll the latex up his hard cock robbed her of speech. Her entire body buzzed with need as she planted her feet on the mattress and lifted her hips high, offering herself to him. Something dark and hungry flickered in his gaze as he grabbed her waist and buried himself inside her, filling her up with one smooth push. Relishing the sense of wholeness she only felt when she was like this with Mateo, she slowly undulated her hips, loving how he fit her in all the best ways, in all the right places.

He groaned and threw his head back as he met her thrust for thrust. Hot. Hungry. Hard. It was always like this between them. Like an explosion just waiting to go off.

The penthouse suite wasn't the draw when it came to Mateo. His body, even as hard and mouthwatering as it was, didn't make her breath catch. It was the confidence in how he moved. It was the raw power that rippled the air around him. It was the way he carried himself, as if nothing bad in the world could touch him because nothing ever had.

It was all of that and something she couldn't put her finger on but it had wrapped around her heart the first time she'd spotted him during a grade-school slumber party at her friend Luciana's house. A part of her had always loved her best friend's older brother and, up until now, having secret fuck-buddy agreement had been enough.

But her life was changing. Fast. Her modeling days were ending and the idea of calm normality didn't scare her nearly as much now as it had when she'd run away from Salvation, promising to never go back.

He plunged into her again and again, as if nothing else in the world existed or mattered. Hands touching. Lips tasting. Bodies moving together. He leaned forward, changing the angle and driving deeper inside, rubbing against her most sensitive spots.

The buzzing started in her calves, gaining strength as it traveled up her legs and spread through her flushed body. Swept along by the overwhelming intensity of sensation, she lost herself to the moment and let her body take her where she needed to go.

"Mateo." She only managed the single word before her orgasm crashed against her, sending shockwaves of pleasure vibrating through her.

Plunging deeper than he had before, he buried himself to the hilt as he cried out his own climax. He collapsed on the bed beside her, pulling her close. Turning her head, she rested her cheek against the smooth expanse of his chest as her breathing slowly came back to normal and the world came back into focus.

When she finally found the energy to open her eyes, he was staring at her with an expression that balanced on the fine line between post-coital awe and something more permanent. He traced his finger across the dramatic rise of her breasts. "God you're beautiful."

Her beauty—and the outrageous behavior she got away with because of it—had always been a tool, a weapon, a wall to hide behind. Men looked at her and saw big tits and a perky ass, but there was more to her than jiggly assets and a wild time. There had to be. If anyone would see that, it would be Mateo.

Grabbing on to her courage before she let the opportunity slip away, the words spilled out of her. "I was thinking that after you got back, maybe we could try this out on a more frequent basis—maybe even go out on regular dates."

His eyes went wide before his gaze skittered away from her. "Olivia..."

An icy wave of disappointment washed over her before a flaming swell of fiery embarrassment threatened to drown her. She'd walked down runways in little more than glittery strings pretending to be a bikini, but she'd never been as exposed as she was right now.

Rolling away from his touch, she sat up and forced her lips to curl into a beguiling half smile that had landed her multiple magazine covers and hidden far more heartbreaks. “Don’t freak out. I’m not talking marriage.”

“We talked about this in the beginning,” he said, his tone soft and too kind. “We agreed to certain boundaries.”

“Things change.” She barely got the words out before emotion pinched her throat shut.

“Not for me.” The gentleness in his voice hurt more than if he’d laughed in her face.

He cared—but not enough.

And she cared too much.

She stood up on shaky legs. “I gotta go.”

Not waiting to see what he’d do—or not do—she rushed into the living room. Her dress lay in a puddle in front of the window. Putting it on took a millionth of the amount of time taking it off had, even with her trembling fingers fumbling the zipper. She hustled to the elevator door and punched the down button. Then pressed it again. And again. And again.

“You need this,” Mateo said from behind her as he slipped his room key into the slot above the button. “I’m sorry, Olivia. I never meant to give you the wrong impression. I’m just an asshole Marine who lives on adrenaline and MREs. I’m not the kind of guy people like you should depend on.”

The elevator doors opened and she hurried inside.

“We had fun, Mateo. Let’s leave it at that and pretend the rest never happened.” Raising her chin, she inhaled a trembling breath as the doors began to close. “Stay safe during your deployment.”

He opened his mouth but the elevator doors closed, cutting off whatever he was going to say.

Olivia sank back against the wall and fought against the tears she refused to shed. She should have known better than to fall for a pretty boy like Mateo Garcia.

She hadn't cried this morning when her modeling agent told her she'd walked her last runway because the trend was for slimmer, less-curvy models. She hadn't cried growing up when practically everyone in her hometown of Salvation had treated her and her family like dirt. And she sure as hell wasn't going to cry now—no matter how much she wanted to.

So she would start her new post-modeling life without the man she loved. She could deal with that. She clamped her jaw tight to stop her chin from trembling and sniffled back the threatening tears. It didn't matter. She'd find the place in the world where she belonged all on her own. No one knew better than a Sweet from Salvation that life rarely *gave* you what you wanted. You had to fight for it.

Chapter Two

Today

Tucking Handsome into her red-and-white polka dot trench coat to protect the overweight three-legged cat from the spring downpour, Olivia Sweet pushed open the door of her bright-yellow Fiat and stepped out onto uncertain terrain. A flash of lighting illuminated the soggy night, followed by a boom that rattled her teeth and scared the bejesus out of the mangy cat, if the claws suddenly embedded like tiny daggers in her boob were anything to go by.

"He empties the bank accounts and the apartment but leaves *you*. What a prince of a douchebag ex-boyfriend." She pried Handsome's razor-sharp claws out of the very flesh that used to pay her bills.

Her back tires mired hopelessly in the mud just off the highway, Olivia looked up the hill toward the dirt driveway leading to Uncle Julian's house on the outskirts of Salvation, Virginia. Even in the limited light from her Fiat's headlights, it was evident that the rain had turned the drive into a squishy, slimy mess.

Great. She had a good quarter-mile walk in this mess, uphill, in the dark, in heels, with a snarling, not-quite-tame L.A. alley cat clutched to her chest, and no one was expecting her. Hopefully her sisters would be happier to see her than Mother Nature, who—it turned out—was a royal bitch.

Grabbing her purse and the keys with her free hand, she slammed the door shut and half slid/half skidded her way up. She'd managed three lurching steps before the thick mud swallowed her canary-yellow stiletto whole. Only the top of her ankle bone poked out of the muck.

It was times like these when only a girl's inner Samuel L. Jackson could fully express her frustration. "Motherfucker."

The shoes that would have been worth some real money if she could find a buyer online were now impractical decoration. Just what she needed more of in her life.

Handsome twitched and made that weird mrowly-cat-growl noise.

"Watch those claws, fur ball, or I'll leave you out here."

The cat hissed.

Olivia balanced her weight on her still-free right foot, flexed her left foot, spreading out her toes inside her Jimmy Choo for a better hold, and tugged her leg upward. The mud released her foot with a wet slurp, but retained custody of her obnoxiously expensive shoe.

As she stood with one leg up like a half-drowned, bedraggled flamingo, another flash of lighting and bang of thunder snapped what was left of Handsome's tentative grasp on reality. The cat lost his shit—clawing and squirming his way free from the confines of Olivia's trench coat.

He perched his fat, furry ass on her shoulder for a heartbeat before using her as a launch pad to propel himself into the darkness.

The force of his leap knocked Olivia off kilter. She whirled her arms around, her heart pounding against her ribs as she fought to stay upright in the slick mud. Backward. Forward. Backward again. The earth and the sky repeatedly traded places. She wibbled and wobbled, clawing at the raindrops for balance before toppling forward.

Faster than a lumberjack called timber, she was face first in the sloppy sludge. The cold, dank mud went up her nose and into her open mouth.

That.

Was.

It.

She propped herself up on her elbows, spit out a mouthful of mud, and wiped the back of her hand across her lips. Handsome was one dead cat. Of course, she'd have to catch the surprisingly fast three-legged monster first.

Rising to her feet, and now covered from nose to kneecaps in muck, she lifted her face to the sky. At least the rain would be good for cleaning her face. The torrent washed over her, taking with it the tension locking her shoulders tight since she'd left L.A. in her rearview mirror. Sure, she was still broke, homeless, jobless and her shithead of an ex had posted naked pictures of her to a revenge-porn site, but at least she would be with her sisters—as soon as she could get her ass up this hill.

Lightning flashed, showcasing the quarter-mile mud pit between the highway and Uncle Julian's house.

Well, almost.

First, she had to slog her way up the driveway.

Girding herself for what would undoubtedly be an ugly trek, she pulled her purse strap tight and flicked off her useless right shoe. Mud and only God knew what else squished between her toes.

"Meow." Handsome strutted over to her—as much as he could with his signature loping style on two front legs and one back leg—and sat down on her bare foot.

She wiggled her toes. "So you figure I'm better than the local wildlife, eh city boy?" Olivia hefted the cat up and tucked him back into the opening of her trench coat. "Don't get too comfy. I'm still mad at you."

His purr vibrated against her damp skin.

Picking her foot placement carefully, she marched forward, intent on conquering the last quarter mile. She'd spent years as a model stomping in five-inch heels down the catwalks in New York and Paris, once in little more than a diamond-encrusted bra and panties. Surely she could manage to overcome a little mud. Using the house's front porch as a beacon, she continued onward and upward.

It wasn't the prettiest sashay she'd ever taken, but eventually she made it to the wraparound porch. She'd no more than squished down one mud-covered bare foot on the wood before Handsome sprung from her hold and scurried away—probably to cleanse himself of his dirty humiliation in private.

If only she could be so lucky. Per usual when it came to being a Sweet in Salvation, she had to take her medicine in public, but she wasn't the same flaky wild child who'd left this place after high school graduation. She was stronger, smarter, more with it—fingers crossed, people would see past the layers of mud and see past the retired model to the real Olivia underneath.

Stopping in front of the door, she took a deep breath and pressed her wet finger to the dry doorbell.

Hands at ten and two and one foot riding the brake, Mateo Garcia rounded the bend on Highway 28. The rainstorm had gone from a low-level pain in the ass to white-knuckle worthy three curves in the road ago.

What he wouldn't give for a Humvee and night-vision goggles. Even on high speed, windshield wipers couldn't keep up. The police-department-issued SUV's tires hydroplaned every time he ran over a puddle. Worse still, he had two miles of twists and turns to traverse before he hit the straightaway into Salvation, Virginia.

"Out-fucking-standing," Mateo grumbled.

His headlights reflected off an abandoned yellow car half a click ahead. The tail end stuck out onto the roadway, forcing anyone driving by to slow down.

His heart clogged his throat, expanding until he couldn't take in any air.

An explosion of lightning lit up the area, showing the rugged Afghanistan countryside instead of Salvation County's lush rolling hills.

Mateo blinked and the raindrops turned into blood splattering against the windshield.

The thunder became an IED explosion, a roar louder than anything he'd ever heard before, followed by a deafening silence.

His team was dead, their bodies torn apart by the blast, and it was all his fault. If he'd followed protocol instead of his gut reaction, Ferrante and the rest of them would still be alive.

A high-pitched whine jerked him back into the present time and location. The scroungy mutt he'd picked up as a favor to his sister, the Salvation Humane Society director, cowered in the passenger seat.

"Just a car stuck in a storm. Nothing to worry about, dog." He reached over and scratched behind the pup's floppy ear, the action calming *his* nerves as much as the dog's, and slowed down to take a closer look at the car as they passed. "Looks like somebody ran into trouble."

The headlights were on. He couldn't see any damage from his angle. Stuffing his jangling nerves into a dark hole, he turned on the cherry tops and pulled the SUV over.

Shining his searchlight at the vehicle, he couldn't see any movement or sign of anyone inside.

He grabbed the in-dash radio. "Dispatch, I've got an eleven-ninety-six on Highway 28."

"I thought you were off tonight, Chief." The Salvation Police Department's lone night dispatcher, Simons, could be heard loud and clear over the static.

"Affirmative."

"No rest for the weary, I see." Simons easily fell into the informal rhythm of small-town policing. "Need backup?"

"That's a negative. Looks like they got stuck and abandoned it." With front tires deep enough in the mud he could only see the top part of the hubcap. How did that even happen? Idiot drivers.

Lightning bounced across the dark sky and the dog whined. “Sounds like you got backup already. Is that the dog from the kill shelter?”

“Affirmative.”

“Dog” wouldn’t have been the first word he’d have used to describe the skittish, forty-pound ball of matted fur. Mateo’s scarred reflection in the rearview mirror snuck into his peripheral vision and he averted his gaze. Not that he had room to talk.

“Be sure to bring him by tomorrow.” Simons sighed. ‘My granddaughter is dying for a dog.”

Mateo nodded. “Ten-four.”

He replaced the radio and leveled an assessing look at the yellow Fiat. The rain had tapered off to merely an annoyance. Pushing open the door, he grabbed his flashlight, holding it close to the base, and stepped out onto the rain-drenched pavement.

Cold spring rain snaked its way down his neck and under his black T-shirt as he approached the car. It was just an abandoned vehicle, not a potential IED, but the double-fisted death grip on his gut didn’t abate. Knowing and *knowing* were two very different things. He tried the handle—locked—and shined his light through the window. The car was empty except for three bright-blue suitcases covered from wheels to handles with some fancy designer logos.

Figures.

He pointed the flashlight up what used to be a dirt driveway and now looked like a good excuse to go mud skiing. Well, that explained how the car got stuck. No way were those tiny tires getting any traction.

Still, he couldn't leave the car's ass out in the road. Another vehicle coming around the bend could easily clip the Fiat's fender and spin out.

Time to break out the hitch and the four-wheel drive. Of course, he needed to make contact with the vehicle owner first.

He pivoted to return to his SUV and his flashlight illuminated the mailbox next to the driveway. Written in bold black letters across the side was a single word.

Sweet.

The Sweet triplets were nothing but trouble wrapped up in bodies built for sin, with smart mouths and quick brains. They'd provided more private torment for men of a certain age in Salvation than there were days in the year. The older two had been in town for months now. Miranda drove a Lexus. Natalie had some fuel-efficient subcompact.

Mateo glanced back at the yellow Fiat with the fancy luggage in the back.

That left Olivia. Just her name was enough to recall the smoothness of her skin, the taste of her kiss...and the look on her face when he'd turned down her offer for a more permanent relationship rather than just a long, hard fuck in a fancy hotel room when their paths crossed.

Now the last woman he'd touched was going to see the beast he'd become.

His gut twisted. Of all the Sweets in Salvation, the car had to belong to Olivia. "What a clusterfuck."

As tempting as it was to drive off, it wasn't an option because even though he hadn't always, he now understood the importance of following the rules—written and unwritten. He'd learned that lesson the hard way and would never forget it again.

Grumbling under his breath, he stormed back to the SUV, yanked the door open, scooped up the ragamuffin pooch and humped it up the driveway.

Her ear still ringing from her sisters' surprised squeals, Olivia emerged from the bathroom with freshly washed feet, her long hair tied back with a borrowed ponytail holder and wearing a dry pair of yoga pants from Miranda and a T-shirt from Natalie.

"The three musketeers, back together again." Miranda handed her a glass of beer from the Sweet Salvation Brewery, which they'd inherited from their uncle, along with the house. "With a few additions, of course."

Logan Martin and Sean Duvin raised their beers in a toast. Logan and Miranda were getting married in a couple of months, and Sean had declared his love for Natalie on national TV. Saying her sisters were off the market was putting it mildly.

And she was the fifth wheel who didn't belong. *Nice.* Unease crept across her skin. "Sorry for crashing the double date. I would have called first but—"

"Don't worry about it." Miranda gave her a quick squeeze. "We know to always expect the unexpected with you."

Right about now, Olivia would sure love a hell of a lot less of the unexpected.

"So what got you here early?" Natalie narrowed her gaze, her blue eyes as questioning as always. "Is everything okay?"

Damn. Natalie never missed a thing.

"Why would you think it's not?" Telling her sisters what had happened was going to be embarrassing enough—nothing like having to admit how low she'd fallen to feel as though she really was the devil-may-care pretty girl who lived off her looks everyone thought she was, instead the motivated woman with a brain she really was. There was no way she'd be spilling her guts in front of the dudely duo of Logan and Sean. "Can't a girl surprise her favorite sisters?"

"We're your only sisters," Miranda deadpanned.

"Lucky me." Even to her own ears, her words sounded strained.

Natalie focused her gaze as if Olivia was a puzzle to be solved. Miranda opened her mouth, no doubt to start the questions, but a sharp rap on the door saved her from a full-on, spotlight-in-the-face interrogation.

"I'll get it." Olivia practically sprinted to the front door. Whoever was on the other side was her new favorite person in the whole wide world.

She flung it open and the chilly wind brought in a smattering of raindrops that pelted her cheeks.

A man holding what looked like the end of a mop—if mops could shiver and whine—stood half in the shadow. The lighting kept his face mostly in the dark, but something about his take-no-shit stance and the breadth of his wide shoulders tickled a memory and jacked up her heartbeat.

"Hello, Olivia."

That voice. Deep and low, it poured over her like warm honey and reignited a fire she'd thought she'd put out years ago. "Mateo."

After his little sister and her best friend, Luciana, had told her about the roadside explosion while he and his team were on some hush-hush mission, she'd left messages at the VA hospital and sent e-mails and care packages. He'd ignored them all. She'd tried to visit but the nurses turned her away, saying she wasn't on his approved visitors' list. After a year, she'd given up. She wasn't the smartest Sweet sister but she wasn't an idiot either. "It's been forever."

"Close to it." His large hand rubbed behind the dog's floppy ear. "That your Fiat at the bottom of the drive?"

"I got stuck." Nodding, she looked past him into the darkness beyond, but her gaze returned to his tall outline and the dripping dog in his strong arms. "Do you want to come in and dry off for a bit?"

His only acknowledgement of her invitation was to take a half step farther outside of the porch light's reach. "You gotta move the car. Another driver could get hurt."

Annoyance flicked her skin. After years as a model, she should be used to people assuming her head held nothing but fluff, but it still rubbed her nerves raw—especially coming from someone who knew better. "You don't think I tried?"

"That would explain why the tires are half-buried." He sighed. "Do I have your permission to tow it out of the mud and onto the shoulder?"

"My permission?"

He stepped forward enough that the light touched his broad chest, and then pulled his jacket open to reveal the Salvation Police Department logo imprinted on the T-shirt. "Yes or no?"

A meow sounded as Handsome wound his way through her legs in figure-eight fashion.

The fat feline temptation proved too much for Mateo's dog. The little guy sprung forward, landing with a wet thump at Olivia's feet.

Handsome hissed and smacked her front paw against the dog's nose before sprinting out into the night.

She grabbed the dog's collar before he could take off after the mean kitty. Handsome might only have three legs, but she still had serious cat ninja skills. The dog's collar abraded her fingers as it twisted in attempt to break her grasp and give chase.

"Here, let me." Mateo stepped forward and scooped up the dog. The movement brought all six-foot, four-inches of him fully into the light.

Her focus followed the dog's course as Mateo lifted it. Past muscular thighs developed on the football field back in the day and honed to perfection in the Marine Corps, over the form-fitting jeans that hugged his narrow hips and perfect ass, and up the T-shirt covered abs that surely were just as delicious as her memory recalled. She closed her eyes, and in that heartbeat, his face flashed in her mind, the square chin, dimple dipping into his left cheek, the hazel eyes that went from hazy green to warm amber depending on his mood.

She'd spent most of the past few years surrounded by gorgeous men in the world, but none had met the Mateo ideal. Really, could anyone compare to a girl's first love?

No.

The certainty of it whooshed through her and she opened her eyes, her gaze firmly on Mateo's face. But it wasn't his face anymore. At least not the one she remembered. Luciana hadn't told her about the extent of his injuries and she hadn't pushed for details—knowing he was alive and doing well was all her heart could take after his no-bullshit brush-off.

But now, she couldn't look away. An angry two-inch-wide scar wound its way across the left side of his face, from his temple to his square jaw, like a crooked river of agony. Most of his left ear was gone and what remained looked as if it had been formed in clay by an angry toddler.

Olivia couldn't stop the surprised gasp that escaped.

Mateo went perfectly still.

Shame set her face on fire. Of all the idiotic responses, she'd had to have the worst. If anyone knew what it was like to have people overreact to how someone looked, it was her. "I'm sorry...I..." She reached out for his hand, but he evaded her touch with the ease of a man always aware of his body in relation to others.

His hazel eyes turned the color of murky river water on a cold morning and a bitter smile twisted his lips.

"Not exactly what you remember, huh?" He turned to fully display the scarred left side of his face to her. "Look your fill. I don't give a rat's ass."

She jerked her chin down so she couldn't see his shredded face. An invisible fist squeezed the air from her lungs and twisted them into knots. The urge to turn and bolt rose up like an undeniable tidal wave pushing at her to just move already. The need to escape the gut-wrenching reality of his pain made her pulse frantic and kept her gaze locked on the porch's floorboards. She'd spent most of her life as the object of rude stares and abject curiosity. How could she subject him to that cruel scrutiny?

She didn't want to look. She wasn't sure she could.

But this was Mateo, and he'd demanded it of her. She had to look, to bear witness. And she would.

Pushing past the whirlwind of emotion, she clamped her jaw tight and lifted her face to give him her full attention.

The right side of his face remained the same as it had been in high school, when she'd sighed after him while Luciana rolled her eyes. High cheekbones, sinfully long eyelashes, a strong jaw and hazel eyes. The Casanova of Salvation, they'd called him back then, and he'd more than earned the moniker.

Taking a deep breath, Olivia moved her gaze to the other half of his face. The left side was a map of devastation with his malformed ear, the tight skin of healed burn scars and the slight droop to his eye.

Seeing the scars, the thick red lines that marred his brown skin, hurt. Not because of the visual he presented, but because she hated that he'd had to go through whatever had done that to him.

Olivia fisted her hands, angered by her inability to offer anything but words to make it better, and took a step closer and reached out again. "Mateo, I—"

He shot her proffered hand a scathing look and edged back. "I don't need your words or your fake pity. I need your damn car out of the road before someone ends up hurt or worse." Contempt lay thick in his tone. "There are things more important in this world than how people look."

She deserved that after her earlier reaction, but it didn't mean she was giving up.

She swiped her keys off the entryway table. "Let me put on my boots and coat."

In a heartbeat, his face transformed into one of patronizing concern. "There's no need to worry your pretty little head about such mundane things as the lives of anyone who may be driving down that road in a rainstorm." He snatched the keys from her grip, his warm fingers setting off an unsettling swirling sensation in her stomach. "I'll leave the keys in your glove box; you can get them in the morning."

With that, he pivoted and stormed off the porch. The squirming dog in his arms howled in protest as Mateo marched down the hill, surefooted and impervious to the pitch dark, the slippery mud, the punishing rain or the wounded woman left in his wake.

Chapter Three

Olivia closed the thick oak front door and knocked her forehead against it three times, hoping to pound the last few minutes from her memory. Like just about everything else in her life right now, it didn't work. She couldn't stop seeing the millisecond of hurt that flashed in Mateo's hazel eyes before the emotion drained out, replaced with a hard-edged bravado. Regret and shame burned through her like battery acid.

"You are a total ass." Miranda echoed the words ringing in Olivia's ears.

Olivia spun on her heel to face her older sister. "Thanks, oh wise one, I hadn't figured that out yet."

They may be only minutes apart in birth order, but Miranda had always been the Type A leader, insisting her way was the only way to get something done. Without meaning to, Olivia slipped back into the role she'd always played when they were growing up: rebellious smartass.

Logan and Sean, obviously sensing a Sweet triplets brouhaha on tap, smartly hung back in the living room, seemingly engrossed in Uncle Julian's erotic sci-fi book collection.

Natalie, ever the middle-child peacemaker, stepped forward to join the fray. "She was just shocked. It wasn't like she meant to hurt Mateo's feelings."

She hadn't, but the end result was that Olivia had made him feel like shit, even if he wouldn't show that to the world. She couldn't let that stand. Even after he'd squashed her heart under his steel-toed boot, he deserved better than her moronic, unfiltered reaction.

"I'm sure the fact that I didn't mean to be a total bitch really makes a difference to him." Olivia grabbed a pair of rubber boots and shoved her bare feet inside the fake-fur-lined interior. "I need to go help move the car. It's the least I can do."

Natalie scrunched her nose, dislodging her glasses and forcing her to push them back up. "I don't think he really wants you around right now."

Wasn't that the story of her life? The town of Salvation didn't want the crazy Sweet family, but she'd grown up here anyway and spit in the eye of anyone who gave her a cross look. The modeling world didn't want her in the beginning because her voluptuous curves didn't fit with the stick-thin catwalk models in New York. One magazine editor had even gone so far as to call a picture of her standing in a bikini "vulgar" because she had big boobs. Internet commentators had called her fat and there were entire thinspiration boards devoted to detailing her supposed faults. She'd refused to back down and had become one of the top-paid models in the industry before the newness wore off and the pendulum swung back to long, lanky, thin models. Then she'd decided to explore the corporate world. She'd retired from modeling, taken a job as a public relations and marketing specialist, found a non-industry boyfriend and rescued the world's meanest cat from a kill shelter.

Okay, that last one hadn't turned out so well since she was now broke, homeless, jobless and her shithead of an ex was posting naked photos of her to revenge-porn websites.

There wasn't fuck all she could do about any of that at this moment, but she could fix things with Mateo. And she would.

She turned, facing both sisters head on. "I made a mistake. I need to make it right. Anyway," she shrugged. "When have I ever done what was expected of me?"

Her sisters stared at her, Natalie pensive and Miranda all judgey. But then, Miranda shook her head and laughed. Tension seeped out of Olivia's shoulders.

"There was that time...no wait, that was Natalie." Miranda reached in the hall closet and retrieved a pair of men's shoes. She tossed them to Logan before sinking her feet into her own. "We'll go with you."

Backup would be awesome, the three musketeers—sort of. Instead of the Sweet triplets it would be Olivia, Miranda and Logan. Not quite the same. She sighed.

God, she should have thought her trip out more before coming home the second the idea hit her. The impulsive, balls-to-the-wall, all-in Sweet DNA ran strong through her veins, but that didn't mean it didn't sour her reality every once in a while.

Time to suck it up and take her medicine by herself. "I appreciate it, but I'm good."

Miranda paused in the middle of yanking up a boot, cocking her head to one side. "Are you sure?"

Surprisingly, she was. "Yeah, I'm a big girl. I can take whatever he's pissed off enough to dish out."

Slip-sliding her way down the steep, muddy driveway, Olivia tried to come up with something to say that would fix what her impulsive first reaction had fucked up. Halfway down the hill, she spotted the glow of headlights in the distance but still had jack shit. Three-fourths of the way down, the light grew to create a warm orange-yellow beacon in the drippy night, but she still had nothing. Zip. Zero. Zilch.

She skittered to a stop a few feet up from the highway and her breath caught.

Mateo stood outlined by his portable floodlight as he bent to hook the towline to the back of her Fiat. Broad shoulders, narrow waist and a butt that was as close to perfect as possible. He'd ditched his jacket and his wet T-shirt clung to him, showing off his back muscles almost as well as if he'd been naked. He straightened and rubbed the back of his neck, the floodlight's beams spotlighting the corded muscles on his forearm, before reaching down for the towline and tugging it to make sure it was secure. The mutt trotted over to Mateo's side and nuzzled his leg.

He looked down and chuckled, the move exposing the scarred left side of his face to the light. "I saw less mud during two government-paid vacations in Kandahar than on you right now." He ruffled the dog's fur.

That self-effacing humor sent her right back to high school. It was one of the first things that had drawn her to him. While the other boys bragged or teased or tried to out-gross each other, Mateo had been cool, confident and at ease with the world. He'd been so focused on accomplishing his mission of joining the Marines and become a recon Marine, the baddest of the bad, that the rest of that cocky-teenage-boy bullshit hadn't seemed to register with him.

What mattered to him now? She wished like hell she knew.

Mateo gave one last tug to the towline, triple checking its security. Old habits, unlike favorite T-shirts, didn't wear out with time.

The line didn't give. Not that he expected it to, but a man like him didn't leave things to chance or things went FUBAR oil-slick fast. A well-timed phantom twinge from his mangled ear reminded him of just how bad the clusterfuck could get. And he was one of the lucky ones.

The dog whined, high-pitched and hopeful, pulling Mateo's focus away from the past and back into the rainy, muddy present. Excited energy had the dog quivering, but the mutt didn't even so much as move a single paw forward.

"What's got you so worked up?" He patted the dog on the head and glanced up the hill, scanning for what captured the dog's attention. That's when he saw her.

Olivia stood just inside the headlight's reach. Tall even in rain boots, she had Jessica Rabbit's curves and full lips that made him wish he was a tube of ChapStick. Fuck, the number of times he'd been tormented by memories of her that had followed him across the globe with every *Sports Illustrated Swimsuit Edition* and *Victoria's Secret* catalog that managed to find its way to whatever hellhole he was in... Getting hot and bothered over her was the last thing he needed. He'd had his chance and he'd run hell-bent for leather in the opposite direction. There was no going back, especially now, when he looked and felt like a dented can of refried beans months past the expiration date

The dog whined, his tail thunking against Mateo's calf. No surprise. Man or animal, everyone seemed to want Olivia Sweet.

Lucky him, he wasn't just another sad sap looking to get in a model's pants. "I told you not to come down here."

She smirked as she pigeon-stepped down the last few yards to his side. "People tell me a lot of things."

"And you never listen." The explosion had fucked with his vision temporarily and his hearing permanently, but not his sense of smell. Right about now, when her flowery scent mixed with the spring rain and warm earth, he wished like hell it had.

"Look, Mateo." She shoved her hands deep into her purple rain jacket's pockets and raised her chin, as if her posturing could cancel out the slight tremor in her husky voice. "I'm sorry."

"For what?" His scar throbbed. He could take the way people's eyes slid away, the nervous chatter and the avoidance. But the pity he saw in her blue eyes? It fucking unmanned him.

"My reaction." Her gaze dropped for a second before returning to lock with his. "I was an asshole."

No excuses. No denial. He shifted his stance, annoyed with the twinge of his conscience.

"Forget it." He shrugged. "Do you really think I give a fuck what people think?"

Her long fingers grazed his soaked T-shirt over his biceps. A bolt of lightning could have struck the tip of his steel-toe boots and it wouldn't have jolted him any more than that single touch. How long had it been since a woman had done that? Used to be he couldn't grab a beer without a long-legged beauty saddling up to him at the bar. Now? Everything was different.

Bitterness ate away at the back of his throat and his pulse jacked up. The last time he went to a bar, he hadn't even gotten a second glance after the wide-eyed shock of the first one.

Olivia squeezed his arm, softly. "I know what it's like—"

"To have half your face blown off and everyone else in your team blown to bits because you failed to follow standard operating procedure? Because you just couldn't believe that the enemy would use a four-year-old child as a trigger to set off a roadside bomb?" Cold and deadly, the words spilled out and he shook off her hand. "You, Miss Prance-Around-In-A-Bikini-For-A-Living, know what *that's* like?"

He expected her to turn tail and run. That's what a normal person would have done. But she didn't. She didn't even flinch. Figured. She was a Sweet, after all.

"No, I don't."

"Then don't bother with the touchy-feely shit. Go back inside." And away from him before he said anything else he shouldn't.

She locked her jaw and crossed her arms. "I'm staying."

Did the woman want to make what was left of his head pop off? "Why?"

"Because I have to." Her gaze dropped to the dog, who promptly starting wagging his tail so hard his whole butt swayed.

Between the dog's insistence on being underfoot and Olivia's stubborn refusal to stop acting like a crazy Sweet, Mateo wondered if he was going to have to stop by the hospital on the way home to make sure he wasn't having a heart attack.

Sometimes even a Marine had to concede the battle to win the war. He rubbed the back of his neck, easing the tension stiffening the IED blast's lingering phantom effects. "Then at least make yourself useful and keep the dog out of the way."

She grinned, the action transforming her pretty face into one that stopped people cold in their tracks. Sinking to her haunches, she made a kissing sound and the mutt, obviously unable to resist any longer, wiggled over with his ears tucked in ecstasy. "What's his name?"

"Doesn't have one."

"You didn't name your dog?"

"He's not mine," he snapped.

With a final sloppy kiss to her hand, the dog scurried back over and sat down on Mateo's right boot.

One eyebrow went up and she snorted. "Sure seems like he is."

"Appearances can be deceiving." The dog's fat tongue lolled out of his mouth. The fuzzy bucket seemed happy enough, but he wasn't about to become a dog owner. His plate was full already and with the Sweet triplets back home in Salvation, things were only going to get worse.

Chapter Four

Still slightly waterlogged from the night before and sore from sleeping on a pullout couch, Olivia opened the door to her new office at Sweet Salvation Brewery, squeezed her hand between a giant cardboard box and the wall and flicked on the light switch.

She immediately wished she hadn't. Brown cardboard boxes started at the green vinyl floor and went up to the ceiling. Stretching her neck, she peeked around the stack closest to the door and spotted a green metal desk covered with more boxes. The musty scent of old papers and forgotten information filled whatever pockets of space weren't taken up by boxes. A defeated groan escaped before she could stop it and she slumped against the doorjamb.

"I'm really sorry about this." Miranda gave her a quick squeeze around the waist. "We've been using this as storage because we thought we had another couple of months before you came home to become the brewery's marketing chief."

"So did I," Olivia muttered as she slipped from her sister's grasp and slid sideways through the maze of boxes to the opening in front of her desk.

No one would confuse this mess for the tenth-floor offices of Matrix Public Relations in Los Angles, but she could make it work. She had to. It wasn't like she had anywhere else to go. The family brewery was all she had left. She pushed a box on top of the desk with her finger. It didn't budge. Maybe she needed to take a lesson from the box.

Her uncle had left her an equal share in the failing brewery, along with her sisters. They'd done their part to get what had been a doomed business back in order, now she just had to figure out how she could be a part of the Sweet Salvation Brewery's turnaround.

Executing a quick spin, she came nose-to-nose with her oldest sister.

"Are you ready to spill?" Miranda gave her a total big-sister-knows-best glare. "I know you were holding back last night."

"You know you're only a few minutes older than me. I don't think that's enough to call seniority."

"It's six minutes and I'm not pulling rank so much as trying to figure out what's going on with you. Last time we talked, it sounded like your boss was insistent on two months' notice before you could leave for good. It wasn't something that loser you were dating did, was it?"

And wasn't that just like Miranda to examine all the angles until she came up with a likely scenario. Salvation was lucky Miranda hadn't been the wild Sweet triplet or the busybodies would have spontaneously combusted from all the gossip she would have generated. As it was, Olivia had caused enough trouble on her own. She'd have to explain everything to her sisters eventually, but not yet. Her sisters had spent a lifetime helping her clean up her messes, this time she wanted to do it herself.

Olivia shrugged off her sister's question. "It's a long story and more appropriate if there's a bottle of wine handy."

"You better not let Sean hear you say that." Miranda giggled. "This is a beer-only zone."

"I'll remember to watch it." Relieved the deflection worked, she scanned the room again, hoping it wouldn't look as bad since the shock had worn off. No such luck. "So where are we going to put all this stuff?"

Natalie poked her head in the room, her glasses askew and her lips swollen. "Give me ten minutes. I just have to grab the charts I made outlining how to label each box and where we'll store them."

Olivia rolled her eyes. "Some things never change."

Sean crossed in front of the open doorway, tugging Natalie along with him. "Make it thirty."

Natalie turned about ten shades of red and waved her fingers at her sisters as she disappeared down the hall.

Or maybe they do. It took a couple of seconds and several slow blinks to get past this latest shock. Who'd have thought the uptight middle triplet would be sneaking off for a little afternoon delight at nine in the morning?

"Close your mouth or you'll gather flies." Miranda shoved a box into Olivia's arms. "Come on, we'll load up one of the delivery vans and take everything over to self-storage."

She snapped her jaw shut hard enough that her teeth clinked. Was nothing the same anymore? Because everything sure looked different. Following her sister out into the hall, Olivia ignored the misgivings making her stomach clench.

"Don't worry, after we get home tonight, we'll find a way to give you some privacy there," Miranda said. "Maybe we can convert the living room to a bedroom with some standing screens. If only Ruby Sue hadn't rented out Sean's old house, but as it is, we're five people in a two-bedroom farmhouse."

"No big deal." The box in her hand felt ten pounds heavier, weighed down by embarrassment about what had brought her to Salvation and elbowing her way into a house filled with couples in love. "I'm sure I'll be able to find some place in town to rent."

Now, how she'd pay for it, *that* was a whole new problem. Until she figured out a way to tell her sisters how her entire life had gone straight to hell in a designer handbasket, laying all of her humiliations bare, she had to act like money wasn't a problem.

Boob sweat was the worst sweat. After almost two hours of moving boxes from her office, beads of perspiration slinked down between Olivia's considerable assets, which just happened to be covered by a bazillion nerves. It took everything she had not to stuff a pound of paper towels down the front of her shirt to end the torture. Only the near-constant presence of Sean kept her from seeking relief. Of course, there was a good chance he'd never notice with the way his eyes stayed glued on Natalie.

"Looks like these are the last two," Natalie said, nodding toward the box she held and the one Sean had. "We'll get out of here and let you get yourself sorted."

"Put that on mine," he said

"I can carry it," she replied.

"Never said you couldn't."

They stared at each other for a moment.

Natalie sighed. "It *is* more efficient for only one of us to make another trip to the truck."

"Yep." He winked and let loose with the grin that had sold millions of movie tickets before he'd run away from Hollywood and found Salvation and Natalie.

She stacked her small box on top of his and followed him out of the office. "It's not fair when you use my methods against me."

The conversation—at least Natalie's part of it—continued as the couple walked down the hall.

The brewmaster might not say much out loud, but his actions spoke volumes. Olivia pursed her lips together and blinked away a few happy tears. Living life as a Sweet in Salvation meant being thought of by most of the town as the craziest of crazy. Most of her family had seen the inside of the Salvation County Jail on more than one occasion. Her grandparents because of prohibition—the brewery, after all, had been started after prohibition as a way to capitalize on their moonshining success. Then there was the time her dad had single-handedly brought the high school homecoming football game to a halt with a protest in the middle of the first quarter. The fact that her sisters had both found love in Salvation was nothing short of a miracle. Even if it meant she'd turned into the fifth wheel, Olivia wouldn't change a damn thing about it.

"Hey, Olivia." The intercom in her office buzzed. "You have a visitor."

"Who is it?"

"What, you too good for an old friend?" Luciana's teasing tone lightened her words. "Get on out here or I'm busting in."

There was no way Luciana needed to be on the other end of the intercom to hear Olivia's squeal as she sprinted down the hallway. E-mails, texts and calls between them tended to be sporadic but as soon as they connected, it was as if a day hadn't passed since high school graduation. Rounding the corner, she spotted Luciana before the other girl saw her. Long brown hair, big brown eyes and enough bright red lipstick to make a Ferrari jealous, Luciana hadn't changed a bit. She squealed again. Luciana did a happy shimmy. Before Olivia knew it, they were hugging it out in front of a bemused Hailey, Sweet Salvation Brewery's office manager.

"I thought you were visiting family."

"Girl, you know I'm good for three days tops with my in-laws."

"Is this Amalie?" Olivia squished her face and made coochie-coo noises at the twenty pounds of chubby baby in the carrier.

"I should smack you for that. This..." Luciana pulled a doe-eyed two-year-old from behind her, "...is Amalie. This..." she nodded toward the baby, "...is Benito, and his machismo demands a proper apology."

"It *is* lunchtime. How about a giant slice of Ruby Sue's pecan pie for mommy to make up for it?" Olivia dropped her gaze to the little girl. "Big enough to share."

"Sounds good. Let me drive. I have the car seats."

The twenty-minute car ride into town was filled with the kind of stream-of-conscious conversation filled with constantly changing subjects and giggling ferociously that only happened with great friends or her sisters. By the time they arrived at The Kitchen Sink Diner, Olivia was up to speed on everything Amalie-related and every last tidbit about Benito's dedication to putting everything in his mouth.

The lunch crowd had begun to peter out by the time she and Luciana strolled through the door with their mini-me-sized entourage. The Kitchen Sink Diner's proprietor, Ruby Sue, sat behind the cash register, her tight-curled hair a tribute to Aqua Net and old-lady perms. She also happened to make the best pecan pie on the face of the earth and had a soft spot for all things Sweet and sweet. A hole inside Olivia that she hadn't realized was empty filled up at the sight of the woman always armed with the sweetest tea this side of the Mississippi. Seeing Ruby Sue was almost as good as seeing her sisters.

"Lookie what the cat dragged in." Ruby Sue slid down off her high perch and came bustling around the counter, smelling of cookie dough and sounding like a six-pack-a-day smoker. "It's about time you showed back up in Salvation. The town was starting to get boring."

As quick with a juicy tidbit as she was with a well-timed barb, Ruby Sue was the living, breathing center of all things gossip-related in Salvation. The town, like all small towns, thrived on knowing everything about everyone, which made The Kitchen Sink Diner the place to be. For the Sweet triplets, it had been a refuge from the town that always looked down on them and their family. Ruby Sue had always been there with a slice of pecan pie and a gruff piece of advice.

Olivia bent down and hugged her own fairy godmother. "Meaning you're looking for fresh gossip."

She cackled and grabbed two menus before making a beeline toward the back of the diner. "Something like that."

"I'll see what I can do," Olivia said.

"Expect nothing less from you. Come on, I have the perfect table."

She, Luciana and the kids followed Ruby Sue's trail through the last vestiges of the lunch crowd. It was hard to miss the pointed stares and whispers from the handful of folks polishing off pie and coffee. She caught snippets of hushed conversation.

"Shouldn't have come back."

"Those Sweets are nothing but trouble."

"She's the trashiest of the whole bunch."

Those who didn't know her better thought it was the cut-throat modeling world that had given her skin as thick as an elephant. In reality, it was having to hold her head high among Salvation's disapproving citizens, most of whom had never met a Sweet they liked or trusted. Her sisters had both fought the crazy Sweet moniker. Olivia had embraced it, which had seemed like the best choice at the time. Now all she could see was the leftover baggage of her decision.

"Damn straight you will liven things up." Ruby Sue made a sharp left around a table of men dressed in head-to-toe camouflage. "Your sisters have gotten downright dull and you always were the wild child."

Olivia glanced over at Luciana, who was half listening to the conversation as she carried Benito and herded a distracted Amalie toward the back corner booth. "I don't know. It looks like my partner in crime may have other commitments."

Her friend nodded. "Yep, these two wake up early and keep me running all day. I'm dead on my feet by nine."

Ruby Sue stopped at the booth. Amalie clapped her hands together, raced forward and clambered across the seat, stopping once she reached the welcoming arms of the man already occupying the booth. Mateo gathered the girl up and gave her big squeeze. The girl disappeared under the table, only to reappear on the booth seat on the opposite side, where she promptly took out her crayons and went to work on The Kitchen Sink's kids' menu.

Olivia's pulse took a nosedive before ramping up to warp speed. She'd never been one of those girls to lose their shit over pictures of hunky guys with cute kids, but damn if he didn't make it look good. Better than good.

While she was in the process of reining in the hottie-inspired overreaction, Mateo looked up. She nearly fell down. The man was fucking lethal. The scars? Once the initial shock had worn off, the attraction had come back as meltingly hot as ever, because it had never been about Mateo's looks. It had been about him. At least, the man she'd known during their hotel nights together.

His hazel eyes narrowed and he looked away, but not before giving her a quick once over that left her weak in the knees.

There had to be something in Salvation's water supply that turned people crazy. That was the only explanation for her Jell-O-kneed reaction to a man who had less than no interest in her and acted as if he couldn't stand her.

Ruby Sue pulled herself up to her full height of five-foot, two-inches and in her best stage whisper, said, "Looks like you need a new partner."

"Don't get any ideas," she shot back. If there was anything that would send her last bit of sanity flailing into a black hole, hanging out with Mateo Garcia would be it.

"I'm always full of ideas." Ruby Sue all but rubbed her gnarled, arthritic hands together like an old-time villain. "You know that."

Her stomach sank like an iron balloon. "And that is exactly what I'm afraid of."

Mateo had never cut and run during a firefight, but the sight of Olivia and his sister together again had him thinking of beating feet out of there. Fast.

Luciana had a solid head on her shoulders and was an outstanding mom, but add Olivia into the mix and God knew what would happen. Hopefully he wouldn't have to bail them out of jail. Again.

Still, the sight of her in a V-neck Sweet Salvation Brewery T-shirt that followed the famous curves that had landed her magazine covers taped to CHU walls from Iraq to Afghanistan had his thoughts turning to another direction totally. A few years ago, when he was nothing but a horny pretty boy who thought the world was his for the taking, he'd almost fallen for it. He'd learned better.

"Hey sis." He dropped his gaze to the menu he knew by heart. "Olivia."

"You don't have to say her name like it's a dirty word, you know." Luciana rolled her eyes and settled Benito, still snug inside his carrier, into the high chair Olivia had moved to their table. "And hello to you, too."

She slid into the opposite side of the booth next to Amalie, who was going to town on the kids' menu. That left Olivia standing awkwardly at the end of the table. There wasn't enough room for her to sit next to Luciana, and he, because someone upstairs held a grudge, happened to have an empty seat right next to him. Out of the corner of his eye, he watched her hesitate, taking in the way she pressed her pale pink thumbnail into the pad of her pointer finger. Press. Release. Press. Release.

The woman should never play poker.

"You gonna sit or you planning to eat standing up?" Ruby Sue asked and poked Olivia's upper arm with the corner of a laminated menu. She dropped the menus on the table. "I'll be right back with some sweet tea."

Rubbing her arm, Olivia sat down beside him. They weren't touching, but in the tiny booth it didn't matter. His whole body went on hyper-alert. The flick of her head as she flipped her hair back. The way she nibbled on her bottom lip as she read the menu. How she relaxed back into the seat as if his presence didn't even register.

Not that it should. And not that he gave a flying fuck.

Sure you don't, Garcia.

He tossed down his menu in disgust. He'd lost his ear, not his balls. Time to man up.

"I didn't think you knew she was back in town," he said to his sister.

"It's Salvation." Luciana shrugged. "My phone started ringing last night with the news. So how did Marna Simons's granddaughter like the rescue dog?"

The image of the six-year-old frozen with fear as the dog snored as loud as a Ma Deuce .50 caliber machine gun flashed in his mind. He and Simons had stood in the middle of the police department's front lobby for twenty minutes trying to get the little girl to approach the dog. All the while, the furry beast slept blissfully unaware that his fuzzy ass was still homeless and probably would be for some time.

"Not at all. The mutt is hanging out at the station until I figure out what we can do about it."

Along with the stench of wet dog. The things he did for his sister and her pet projects. Of course, he'd learned as a child that while he may be the older sibling, it was no use arguing with his baby sister once she made up her mind.

"Maybe you can train him to be a service dog for the police department."

Luciana's voice didn't carry a trace of cunning, but his big-brother FUBAR alert was already blasting an alarm. When he'd started picking up stray dogs from the kill shelter for her, he'd told her in no uncertain terms that he wasn't about to keep one.

He sure as shitting wasn't changing his mind. "The only thing that mutt is good for is chewing things he shouldn't."

"Your shoes?" Olivia asked, an amused smile curling her full lips.

His combat boots had made it through several tours but not one night with the mutt. "Yep."

"You know, I bet he'd be a good mascot for the veterans' center," Luciana said. "Maybe you could raffle him off to raise money. With the caveat that he'd have to go to a good home, of course."

"Obviously you haven't set eyes on the dog." Or fought for air because of the fart missiles it fired.

Ruby Sue returned with a waitress who carried three tall glasses of sweet tea on her tray. The waitress dropped off the tea before going to help another table, but Ruby Sue stuck around. He'd have to be a complete idiot not to realize she was looking for a little gossip.

Either oblivious or purposefully ignoring the situation, Olivia took a long drink of sweet tea. Her pink tongue snuck out to swipe away the droplets from her lips, an act that left his mouth dry.

She wiped the corner of her mouth with a paper napkin. "He's a cute dog."

He snorted. "In what universe?"

"If he's as ugly as all that, he'd fit in perfectly at the veterans' center, considering what a wreck it is," Ruby Sue groused. "Just disgraceful what they've let happen."

Olivia looked from Ruby Sue to him to Luciana. "What happened to the center?"

"Remember that big old oak tree at the corner of Main and Rogers?" Luciana asked while retrieving a crayon from under the table that Amalie had dropped.

Olivia nodded.

"Lightning strike hit it and sent it straight through the center's roof." She handed over the crayon and ruffled the girl's long brown hair. "For the past two years, local veterans have been using the courthouse annex until they can raise enough money for repairs."

Packed in like sardines, more like it. Guys came in for help filling out VA forms, navigating the system, connecting with old buddies and networking for post-military careers. The veterans' center was more than just a bar and a hangout. It was HQ.

"But so many people use that facility. Almost everyone in town has two or three family members either going in, on active duty or retired from the military." She turned her blue-eyed gaze on him. "Can't the county help out? Or the federal government?"

Like he was in charge of the county's money instead of police chief of Salvation's six-person force that included two part-time officers. "You may not have realized it, being a rich supermodel and all, but money's tight for most people around here, and tax revenue is down so the county's out and, because it's not an official VA center, the feds don't care about it either."

Luciana kicked him in the shin under the table. Her shoe connected with the bone right under his kneecap with enough force to snap his mouth shut before he could say anything else. The stop-being-an-asshole look on her face was just the exclamation point on her message.

Olivia ignored the scuffle and continued. "What about a fundraiser? The brewery could host one." She unzipped her giant orange purse and started digging through it. "Maybe make it an in-house brew crawl with folks signing up to taste all of the different beers." She pulled out a small notebook and pen before flipping open the cover and writing First Annual Veterans Brew Crawl across the top in big, loopy letters. "We could even call in some of the other craft breweries in the area and have a beer-off."

"What's a beer-off?" Luciana asked.

"I don't know yet, but I'll figure it out." She grinned. "Want to help?"

"I'd love to, but I'm wall-to-wall already." She turned to Mateo, an ornery grin on her face, and his gut tightened. "But you'd be happy to help, wouldn't you?"

If by "happy" she meant dead set against it. The extra sparkle in her eyes said otherwise. "Forget it, sis." He would have sprinted from the booth if Olivia wasn't the one between him and freedom.

"No way." Luciana shook her head and crossed her arms. "You've been holed up in your house by yourself for too long."

He liked his house. It was quiet. People left him alone. No one stared. "I work."

"Exactly." His sister tossed up her hands. "You work, go home and then go to work again. You need to get out."

"I appreciate the thought, Luciana," Olivia sputtered as she pressed her thumbnail into her finger. "But I don't think it's a good idea."

"It is the perfect idea." Jaw set, Luciana eyeballed him before turning her stony gaze to Olivia. "You..." she pointed at Olivia, "need someone to rein in your crazy. And you..." she glared at Mateo, "...need to stop hiding in your man cave and spend some time in the civilized world."

"I'm not hiding." He couldn't stop the words, even knowing they were totally futile. If he didn't do it, Luciana wouldn't stop bugging him about it. She'd push and she'd push and she'd push until he either spontaneously combusted or gave in. Either way, she'd win.

Luciana crossed her arms. "It's decided."

It may be decided, but that didn't mean he had to like it, and judging by Olivia's stick-up-her-amazing-ass posture, he wasn't alone. He shook his head. Despite everything, he was on the same side of an argument with Olivia Sweet. Someone up there really did hold a grudge.

"And it'll be perfect to have you working together since Olivia will be staying at Dad's old cabin behind your house."

Mateo's stomach dropped to his toes. "What?!"

"Luciana," Olivia squealed. "I can't do that."

After his parents divorced, his dad had built a small cabin/guest house on the back of their property and lived in it while Mateo, Luciana and their mom had lived in the house. It had been vacant since his dad retired to Texas. Still, there was no way he could live half a football field away from Olivia and hold on to what little bit of sanity he still had left when it came to her.

"Everyone in town knows your sisters, Sean and Logan are all shacked up together at your uncle Julian's old house," Luciana said. "That place isn't big enough for five people and the cabin is just sitting empty waiting for you."

Olivia shook her head, the light-brown waves turning golden in the afternoon sunlight slanting in through The Kitchen Sink's windows. "I don't think—"

"And forget about rent. My brother, the hermit, has been renovating the bathroom for the past three months but the only progress he's made is to yank out the shower. That mean's you'll have to trudge across the backyard to use the shower in the main house, so there's no way we could charge rent. It's perfect."

Sharing a bathroom with Olivia. Giving her free rein to come in his house whenever she wanted. His brain immediately conjured an image of her in the barely there, see-through lingerie she'd worn at the hotels they'd stayed at—but instead of a five-star hotel, he imagined her wearing it in his house, his shower, his bed. His cock liked the picture. Liked it enough that Mateo had to shift in his seat to accommodate its thickening length.

"Do I have any say in this?" he grumbled.

True to her bulldozing form, Luciana just shrugged. "Dad left the cabin to me, so I can let whoever I want stay there, and you wouldn't leave her to wash in the creek out back, would you?"

"Luciana, it's sweet of you to offer but I'm not sure it's a good idea." Olivia's cheeks had turned pink—the same shade they got whenever he had started talking dirty, telling her exactly how he was going to touch her, lick her and fuck her until she came so hard she couldn't move.

Looked like he wasn't the only one remembering old times.

He caught a glimpse of his twisted reflection in the metal napkin dispenser on the table. The sight was like having a gallon of ice water dumped over his head. She wasn't getting turned-on. Olivia was embarrassed because she didn't know how to say no to his sister's offer.

The perverse urge to have her stay in the cabin fifty yards from his back door took hold of him with a steel grip. The pretty Olivia and the beastly him. Having to see the disappointment and revulsion in her eyes every time she looked at him would be just the punishment he needed to pay for the sin he'd committed against his team by living when they'd all died.

"This place comes totally furnished—including a bed—just minus a shower. And have you looked at the rental market in Salvation lately? It's awful." Luciana continued her verbal battle. "Anyway, if you don't say yes, I'll just keep nagging until I wear you down."

Looking at Olivia, knowing he'd walked away from her before the explosion and that she'd never want him after, hurt him in a way he couldn't even begin to describe—even if he *had* been that sort of touchy-feely bullshit kind of guy. But the pain was good. It was real. As long as he ached, he wouldn't forget the Marines...the friends...he'd left behind.

He turned toward Oliva, the move bringing his knee into contact with hers. Something sparked in her blue eyes, but she dropped her gaze before he could figure out what. Disgust, no doubt.

"Luciana's right," he said. "The cabin *is* perfect. I'll even help you move in."

Ignoring the unspoken question making his sister's eyebrows arch, he downed the dregs of his lukewarm coffee and hoped like hell he hadn't just made another life-altering mistake.

Chapter Five

The paper straw wrapper crinkled between Olivia's fingers as she refolded it for the fifth time in the ten minutes since Luciana had left The Kitchen Sink with her sleepy kids. Like an idiot, she'd stayed behind in the vain hope she could actually work with Mateo the Surly. She'd switched sides in the booth so she sat opposite him and then held an entire brainstorming session for the fundraiser by herself. She'd talked, thrown out ideas, wondered aloud—he'd glared at his coffee mug.

Awkward didn't even begin to cover it.

Walking on the beach in January in heels and a dental-floss bikini for her first *Sports Illustrated* cover? That was awkward. Having to tell her ultra-conservative boss at her first non-modeling job that her douche of an ex-boyfriend had posted pics of her playing with her tits to a revenge-porn site? Most definitely awkward. Meeting her sisters' true loves for the first time while covered head to toe in mud? Totally awkward.

Sitting here trying to pull words, let alone ideas, out of Mr. Grumps-A-Lot bypassed all of that. She'd nearly bitten her tongue off in an effort not to call him on his silent and glowering bullshit. Judging by his attitude, he bore some inner scars to go with the one's crisscrossing the left side of his face, but damn, a woman could only gnaw the inside of her cheek to stop from screaming for so long before she ended up with a hole in her face.

The waitress paused by the table, ticket in hand. "Can I get you folks anything else? How about a free refill?"

"No." Mateo didn't bother to look up or even make a pretense at civility.

The waitress blinked her wide eyes a few times, slid the ticket to the middle of the table and skedaddled away.

Screw this. The man had gone from gregarious heartthrob to man most likely to hit you with the gigantic chip on his shoulder. How in the hell she'd ever fucked him on a semi-regular basis—let alone fallen in love with him—mystified her. There were snarling beasts she'd rather work with more than Mateo Garcia. In fact, she had. She'd done a magazine photo shoot with a lion. The big cat's teeth had looked eight-feet long when she'd snuggled up to him, but it had still been a pussy cat compared to Mateo.

"This isn't going to work." Olivia crumbled the straw wrapper and stuffed it under the corner of her plate. "Let's agree to let Luciana think we're working together on the fundraiser..."

That got his attention. His head snapped up and his hazel eyes sizzled with a dark intensity that made her breath catch. "But we won't be." He finished for her.

"Nope." She grabbed the ticket, completed a quick tip calculation and doubled it as way of an apology for Mateo's attitude.

His large hand engulfed the coffee mug as he lifted it for a drink, every motion measured and efficient. Then he set it back down on the saucer without even the slightest clink. "You think you can just put together an event all by yourself?"

"Absolutely." Flaming lava sizzled through her veins. He could push all he wanted; she'd never backed away from a challenge or a dare. She'd *earned* her reputation as the wild Sweet triplet.

He shook his head, not even a single strand of his dark-brown hair moved out of line. It was as if his entire self—not just his abs—was carved out of granite. "Good luck with that."

She raised her chin and stared him down just like she had every handsy photographer who thought she was too dumb to realize he didn't need to feel her up to get the right shot. "You don't think I can do it?"

The bastard didn't even blink. "Negative."

Anticipation pushed her forward in her seat. Oh, this was going to be classic. "Why not?"

His gaze dropped down to the deep V of her cherry-red top and the pulse in his temple pulsed. For a second she didn't think he was going to say anything, which was good because she'd just forgotten her own name. His focus inched northward across her generous cleavage, up her neck and to her lips—leaving a heated trail across her skin without ever making a move. The last dry spot on her panties surrendered.

"Why not?" He dropped his attention back to the coffee mug in his white-knuckled grasp. "Because you're all unicorns and rainbows and puffy pink clouds."

"What does that even mean?" Besides the fact that Mr. Tough Recon Marine had watched a few too many Disney movies.

"That this is a job that takes organization." He flipped up a finger. "Discipline." Up went finger number two. "And follow through." A third popped up. "None of which are your strong suits."

She didn't need to count off with three fingers in response to his ridiculousness. She only needed one—but she kept that middle finger sheathed. Instead, Olivia added enough sugary sweetness to her voice to knock Mateo into a diabetic coma.

"It also takes creativity and a willingness to try something new—not to mention something more than a piss-poor attitude and a cute butt."

He smirked. "Don't be so hard on yourself. At least you have the hot-ass part down pat."

And to think she'd cried— *cried*—over him.

He reached to pull the bill from her grasp.

She swiped it away before he could get it and slid across the booth. Her bank account balance may be pathetic, but there was no way he was buying her lunch. She wasn't about to owe him anything. "Well, don't worry. You don't have to put up with my questions or idiotic attempts at putting together a fundraiser that would actually help this community. And I'll find somewhere else to shower so I won't be darkening your doorstep."

His hand clamped down on hers, setting off an electric jolt that went straight to all the places it shouldn't. "We're in this together."

"Why?" Now that came out shakier than it should have.

"Because I gave Luciana my word that I'd help you with the fundraiser, and I always keep my word. Always. Come on, I'll drop you off at the brewery." He tugged the bill free from her grasp. "I'll meet you at the veterans' center at ten a.m. tomorrow, then you can see for yourself that this project is too much for you."

Since Olivia's office at the Sweet Salvation Brewery looked like Armageddon at the dust bunny convention, she marched down the hall to Miranda's. Her oldest sister's office was all chrome and dark wood—perfect for the fast-rising Harbor City business executive she'd been before they'd inherited the brewery from their crazy uncle Julian. The only thing that kept the office decor from perfectly toeing the company line was the Live Free, Die High poster leftover from when their uncle ran it.

Miranda and Natalie were hunched over the desk going through paperwork that Olivia would bet dollars to stilettos was some organizational plan the efficiency expert middle triplet had come up with to squeeze an extra half percent of productivity out of the brewery.

While Miranda and Natalie were the exceptions to the all-Sweets-are-crazy rule, she was the Sweet who proved the rule. Still, when she needed to bitch, there was nothing like the triad.

Miranda looked up from the paperwork on her desk. "You look like you're about to set fire to the place. Lunch didn't go well?"

"Lunch was fine; it's Grumps Garcia who isn't." She flopped down into the seat next to Natalie, who hugged her beloved clipboard tight. "Why did I let Luciana talk me into moving into the cabin behind his house?"

"What?" Both sisters exclaimed at the same time, their identical blue eyes round with surprise.

God, she really needed to think before she spoke. That was *not* how she wanted to drop the news to her sisters. "No offense, but Uncle Julian's just doesn't have the space for one more person."

There, that totally sounded better than "my best friend offered up the cabin behind her super-hot brother's house and my hormones wouldn't let me say no, even though I should have because he is a total ass."

Ass. Oh God, his was still amazing. It filled out his uniform pants like they'd been custom made. She shifted in her seat, pressing her thighs together as discretely as possible. *Crap! Stop thinking about Mateo's ass.*

"We'll make room at the house," Miranda said. "We always find a way."

Here her sisters were trying to clean up her mess of a life, just like when they'd been growing up, and all she could think about was Mateo. You could take the girl out of Salvation, but you really could never take the Salvation out of the girl.

"True, but the cabin is already there," she said. "It's vacant. Plus Luciana won't charge me any rent."

Natalie's eyes narrowed. "Why are you worried about paying rent?"

She dropped her chin to her chest. What was that she'd *just* told herself? Oh yeah, no talking without thinking.

"Spill it, Olive Breath," Miranda said.

Oliva sighed. Time to put all of her humiliations out on the table. "I lost my job."

"I thought you'd quit," Natalie said.

"They *asked* me to quit—but that's not all." Olivia slumped back against the chair, taking a second to gather all the pebbles that had been glued together into a giant boulder that had rolled over her life and smashed it to bits. "I made some really crappy investments and lost most of what I'd made modeling, which wasn't a shit-ton to begin with because you don't even want to know the number of times when a designer paid in clothes instead of cash. So I'd gotten the marketing job to pay my bills, never worrying about the morals clause in the contract."

Her chest tightened and she swallowed back the bile thinking about her ex always brought up. "Have either of you heard of My Ex's Pics?" She paused while her sisters shook their heads. "Me neither, until my then shitball of a live-in boyfriend, Larry, posted naked pictures of me to it. I can't get the site's owner, some assprick who hides behind a fake name, to take them down and my lawyer says everything was totally legit because I gave the pictures to Larry as a gift and he, in turn, sold them to this revenge-porn site."

Tits and ass. She could never get away from being more than two boobs and a butt for some men. Sure, she'd chosen to go into modeling, but that didn't mean there wasn't more to her than how she looked. "I had to tell my very conservative boss about the photos. He made noises about how sorry he was as he handed me a box to put all my stuff in and asked for my key to the office back." Anger, white-hot and immediate, burned its way up from her toes. "I went home ready to murder Larry and let the jury fry me if they wanted, but our condo was empty. He'd liquidated everything in our bank account. He'd sold all our furniture plus most of the designer clothes I still had from the old days and then disappeared off the face of the earth. Turns out he owed some bad people a lot of money and when my investments went south, so did his credit rating with the bookie, so he didn't have any use for me anymore and he'd skipped—which turned out to be lucky for me, because I'd look like shit in an orange jumpsuit doing twenty to life for murdering the bastard."

She barely had time to suck in a shaky breath before her sisters' arms were holding her tight, squeezing away all of the bad things she'd experience, all of the hateful words burned into her memory and all of the heartbreaking disappointments that she'd left unsaid. Things may have changed for her sisters, with their new focus on the brewery and their boyfriends, but one thing hadn't—the bond of the Sweet triplets. No one and nothing could tear that apart.

Olivia hadn't realized just how much she'd missed being with her sisters until that moment. She returned the hug before Miranda and Natalie took their seats again.

"So here I am, the crazy Sweet triplet who fucked up her world all over again." She gave a hoarse chuckle. "Just like when I brought the documentary crew home with me one Christmas and left before New Year's with practically the whole town waving pitchforks and burning torches in my rearview mirror."

Now *that* had been a disaster. She'd meant to bring positive attention to the small town and had ended up making it a laughingstock—especially the mayor.

"Your world is not fucked-up," Natalie declared. "It's just Sweet-i-fied."

"You're home now and everything is going to work out." Miranda rubbed her stomach and her gaze turned soft when she glanced at the framed photo of Logan on her desk. "I know it doesn't seem like it but we Sweets seem to find our happy endings in Salvation. You'll find yours too."

"Tell that to Grumps Garcia," Olivia said.

"Oh God, what did you do to offend Mateo now?" Natalie asked as she smoothed back a stray hair that had the gall to escape from her bun.

"Me?" Oh that was rich, considering his snarly attitude about everything. "What makes you think I did anything?"

Both sisters stared at her for a second, slack-jawed.

"You *are* the girl who told a certain short movie star with cultish leanings that you'd rather eat nothing but broccoli for the rest of your life than audition to play the part of his real-life wife." Miranda laughed. "Face it, Olive Breath, you aren't known for keeping your tongue."

She shivered at the memory. That had been one of her better escapes. One of the benefits of growing up a Sweet was being able to spot the unhinged from ten-thousand paces. "True, but I mean come on. Mateo acts like he's still pissed he bailed Luciana and I out of jail for egging the principal's house."

"He did bail you two out for that," Natalie said.

She threw up her hands in the air. "A decade ago!"

Obviously unimpressed with her dramatics, her sisters just shrugged.

Okay maybe she deserved that, but Olivia knew she could do this. She could put together a fundraiser that would knock Salvation back on their heels, raise money for a good cause and help promote the brewery—no matter what Grumps Garcia said. "I'm not a unicorn-loving flake."

Miranda squished up her face in confusion before letting out a deep breath. "No one said you were. You're just...free-spirited."

"Well, I come by it naturally. I am a Sweet, after all. The last in a long line of moonshiners, cattle thieves, and ne'er-do-wells." The words didn't come out as confident as she'd wanted. Her conversation with Mateo had obviously torn off the scab from a wound she thought was long healed.

She and her sisters had different defense mechanisms for dealing with Salvation's massive 'tude about the Sweets. Miranda had become a super-achiever and Natalie had compartmentalized everything, but Olivia had embraced the crazy—at least on the outside. The one who never backed down from a dare. The kid who would try anything once. The girl most likely to do...well...anything. Still, she couldn't help but wonder what life would have been like if she hadn't been a member of one of the most despised and yet gossiped-about families in town.

"Speaking of our long and illustrious line." Miranda turned a soft shade of pink. "I'm pregnant."

The words sank in slowly, like a feather in quicksand.

Baby? A niece? A nephew? The idea settled, took root and filled her up, making her chest expand with love until it nearly burst. A baby!

Miranda's grin was wide enough to show every tooth in her mouth. "Well, aren't you going to say anything, aunties?"

Everything sped back up to normal speed and she launched herself at Miranda, wrapping her arms around her sister and hugging her close and jumping up and down. Natalie joined in a second later. Dogs three counties away had to have heard the Sweet triplets's squeals because within a minute, half the brewery's staff was spilling in through the doorway.

Sean elbowed his way to the front of the crowd. "What's wrong?"

"Absolutely nothing," Miranda said. "I'm pregnant."

"Congratulations." He gave her a quick hug. "Now *that'll* give 'em something good to talk about at The Kitchen Sink."

Ice washed through Olivia's veins. Talk? Oh yeah, there'd be tons of talk, and everyone in town would be watching. The baby's last name would be Martin, but Salvation had a long enough memory to still think of him or her as a Sweet.

Olivia couldn't let this baby grow up like she and her sisters had, in a town where his or her heritage was despised.

She had to change the way Salvation looked at the Sweets, and the veterans' center fundraiser would be the first step in that. It would show the town that the Sweets really could be a power for good. But first she had to get Mateo on board and involved for real. If she couldn't convince him that the Sweets could help the community, then she'd never get the rest of Salvation on board and the baby growing in Miranda's belly would pay the price. Olivia refused to let that happen.

Operation Grumps Garcia would commence as soon as she moved into the cabin behind his house.

Mateo stood in his darkened second-floor bedroom, feeling like a peeping-Tom voyeur but unable to look away as he watched out the window and as light after light flickered on in the cabin behind his house. She'd arrived just before dusk and unloaded a piddling amount of stuff—a few suitcases and a three-legged cat that yowled as if its other legs were being pried off with a pair of rusty pliers. Good thing Luciana had the dog, or the mutt would have howled at his fuzzy nemesis and blown Mateo's cover straight to hell.

The cabin was small—one bedroom, one bath, an eat-in kitchen and a living room. His dad's wondering eye, which had ruined his marriage, had disappeared the moment his mom had served him with divorce papers and he'd moved into the guest cabin behind the main house. The old man had a thing for wanting what he couldn't have. Now wasn't that something father and son had in common?

Olivia moved to the large window in the bedroom and stared out. Mateo slunk back from the window far enough that he wouldn't be seen but not so much that he couldn't watch her. Just because he was acting like a perv didn't mean he wanted her to *think* he was a perv.

She reached for the hem of her T-shirt, inching it upward over her smooth stomach. Then she dropped it as if the material had burned her, reached up and closed the curtains.

Had she seen him? Not possible, but she couldn't have missed that a good dozen windows in the main house looked out straight at her cabin. What she couldn't know though is that the light in her bedroom made a perfect backlight, outlining her every luscious curve against the curtains.

She lifted her T-shirt over her head and dropped it to the floor. He may only be able to see a dark shadow of her form, but he didn't need a clearer picture to remember the way her hips flared out from her small waist or how soft her skin felt under his rough fingers. In the cabin across the yard, with its wildflowers starting to bud, she shook out her wavy hair and lowered her hands. He held his breath as he watched her black outline shimmy her form-fitting jeans over her hips and down her long legs. She still wore underwear, something frilly and lacy and minuscule no doubt; he couldn't see it because of the curtain but he knew she wore it. He'd remember her lingerie addiction for as long as he could recall the feel of her underneath him as he slid his hard cock home inside her—forever. There was a list a country-mile long of things he'd like to forget, but the memories of fucking Olivia weren't on it.

One of his favorites had started with a strip tease and ended with her tied to a chair. He slipped his hand under the elastic waistband of his basketball shorts and gripped his rock-hard cock, stroking slow and steady as he closed his eyes and brought the memory into clear focus.

Miami. Summer. The hotel room had a balcony that overlooked the miles of crowded beaches. He never got a single grain of sand between his toes, though; everything he wanted was in his hotel room.

Olivia sat on a thick cotton beach towel stretched out over a chair on the balcony. Her legs were splayed open, the belts from the hotel robes wound around each of her shapely calves, binding each one to a chair leg. It was the only material touching her soft skin.

"This is what you get for teasing me with that strip-and-run-away routine," he's said. "Now you're mine to play with right here in front of everyone."

Only their shoulders and faces were viewable over the top of the solid balcony up on the twentieth-floor, giving her an exhibitionist thrill without a significant risk of getting caught.

"Now..." He lounged against the small table on the balcony and reached for the bright-red shopping bag with The Treasure Box written across it in fancy script. "What did you bring back from your shopping trip?"

He pulled out an eight-inch pink silicone rabbit-style vibrator. "I hope you got batteries."

"Do I look like the kind of girl who'd forget something like that?"

No, she looked like sin and salvation disguised as the hottest woman he'd ever touched.

Keeping his gaze locked on her as he fished around inside the bag, his hand brushed up against a package of batteries. "That's my Olivia."

He had it loaded in less time than he thought possible but longer than she wanted, judging by the way she squirmed in the chair.

"What's wrong, sweetheart? Does your pussy need some attention?"

"Yes."

"Open your mouth." He slid the vibrator inside. "Suck it; take it deep just like you're going to take my hard cock later."

It disappeared into her mouth as he lowered the back of her chair so she lay flat with her legs secured and her feet flat on the floor.

"Raise your arms up and hold on to the chair. Don't you dare let go." He withdrew the vibe from her mouth.

"What if I do?"

He settled back on his haunches, putting him as close to eye level with her wet pussy as possible. Her pink lips were slick and swollen with need already. Just how he liked her. "You'll miss out on one hell of an orgasm."

"We can't have that."

"Glad we agree." He pressed the vibrator against her opening and inched it forward. "I love watching you take this in almost as I love watching my big cock sink inside you." He eased it out. "Now that *is wet." Bringing it close to his nose, he inhaled. "You smell so sweet." He dragged his tongue up the silicone length, licking up her juices. "And you taste so fucking good that I'm jealous of a sex toy." He pressed it against her opening again, feeling the slight resistance of her tightness before it slid inside. "But not enough that I don't want to watch you up close and personal as you come all over it."*

That's when he pushed it as far as it would go and turned on the dual vibration motors—one that made the part inside her push against her G-spot and the other that rubbed and flicked her clit.

"Oh my God." She arched her back and her legs strained against the bindings.

"That's it; show me how good it feels." He rolled his thumb across the speed control.

She held on to the chair with a white-knuckle grip.

"Look how you tighten your hold on this fake dick. That feels so good, doesn't it, baby? How about when I do this?" He tilted his wrist so the tip of the vibrator rubbed harder against her G-spot.

"Mateo!" Her cry came so loud it had to have carried down to the beachgoers but she was too far gone, too close to the end to care.

Seeing her thrash as she balanced on the threshold of orgasm, as much as she could in her restrained position, had pre-come dripping from the tip of his cock, but he wanted to send her over the edge first. Lowering his head so his face was between her legs, he laved her swollen clit, his tongue rubbing against the buzzing part of the vibrator pressing on one side of her sensitive nub, pushing it harder against her.

Breaking the rules, Olivia released her hold on the chair and grabbed his hair, pressing him against closer to her core. Her climax hit like a tidal wave against his tongue.

Sitting back, he watched her body melt against the chair in the warm Florida sunshine.

The memory of her face as she came back to herself, the absolute ecstasy followed by that look in her eye—the one he hadn't realized until too late meant so much more, sent him over the edge as he stroked his cock. He came hard and sudden, spurting over the top of his hand and splattering against the inside of his basketball shorts.

He grabbed the T-shirt hanging on the back of a chair and wiped his hand clean as he looked out the window at Olivia's cabin. While he'd been jerking off, she'd turned out the lights and disappeared from view.

It was a good thing he had the memories because it was as close as he'd ever get to touching her again—and that was for the best. He didn't need her kind of trouble in his life.

Chapter Six

Mateo stopped dead in his tracks in front of the Salvation Police Department the next morning. The mangy dog Luciana had dropped off earlier was inside losing his mind, spinning and scratching at the Salvation Police Department's glass front door. His unshorn nails clicked the glass as Mateo stood on the opposite side armed with a dozen donuts and the largest coffee he could buy at Heaven Sent Bakery. He'd walked the three blocks down Main Street to the station, ignoring the uncomfortable glances and less-than-covert stares from the people he'd grown up with, so the mutt's happy-to-see-you spaz attack halted Mateo's movements.

"Probably smells the donuts," he muttered to himself as he balanced the box and coffee in one hand and reached for the door handle.

As he pulled it open, he angled his body to protect the donuts. Simons would give him the stink eye for the rest of the day if he lost her morning double-chocolate almond bear claw to the dog. He'd gotten the door open about two inches before the pooch barreled out, jumping and yipping as if he had more than a snowball's chance in hell of getting a treat.

Enacting evasive measures, Mateo executed a quick spin and slid through the doorway. Not realizing that it wasn't wanted, the dog trotted in behind him and followed him across the lobby and through the Employees Only door.

"He's been manning a post at the door all morning," Simons said as she rose from her desk and took the donut box from his grasp.

"Probably planning his escape."

The dog plopped down on his right boot, panting happily with his fat tongue hanging out of his mouth.

"Uh-huh." She took her bear claw and glanced down at the mutt. "He looks like a cagey one."

Wet or dry, the dog looked bedraggled and pitiful. Made up of so many breeds mixed into one shaggy body, he was practically a freak of nature.

"He looks like he needs a bath and probably a bunch of shots."

"What he needs is a name," Simons said, and gave him a pointed stare.

Oh no. You name it, you bought it. He knew the rules. "Why are you looking at me?"

"Because he picked you."

Mateo yanked his foot out from beneath the dog's butt and pivoted on his heel. "Then he's bound to be disappointed." Without waiting for a response, he marched into his office and shut the door behind him. He hadn't even crossed the room to his desk before the mutt started whining and scratching on the other side of the flimsy wood.

First he gets dragged into helping Olivia Sweet with a fundraiser and now a dog was stalking him. Did life get any better? Shit was getting FUBAR fast.

Lucky for him, he'd figured out a way out of the fundraising fiasco. It hit him at about three in the morning while staring at his ceiling, so he wouldn't close his eyes and see Olivia's amazing tits. He'd find plenty of stuff at work to do so he'd be too busy to do any more than the absolute minimum. If that meant showering and being out of his house at dawn and not getting home until after dark, so be it. Extra patrols had to be needed somewhere. Whatever it took, he'd limit his interaction with the crazy woman as much as possible while still keeping Luciana from getting on his case.

He glanced down at the call sheets from the night before. All two of them. Staying balls-to-the-wall busy in a town the size of Salvation wouldn't be easy, but he'd been in worse scrapes.

"Semper fi, do or die," he muttered to the empty room.

A low growl sounded outside his door, followed by a sharp rap.

"Come in."

Salvation's mayor, Tyrell Hawson, pushed the door open. The dog galloped into the room, skidding to a stop beside Mateo's desk. After a quick glance back at Mateo, the mutt returned his focus to Hawson. There wasn't any growling, but the fur on his back stood straight up so there was no mistaking the animal's opinion of the mayor. Maybe the dog wasn't as dumb as a box of rocks after all.

"Mayor."

"Garcia."

He didn't get up. "Is there something I can do for you, Mayor, or did you just come by for a donut?"

Not noticing the slight, Hawson flopped down into the worn guest chair opposite Mateo's desk. "I'll grab one on the way out, but I needed to chat with you a bit first."

"Shoot."

"I understand that Olivia Sweet is in town. Possibly for good."

Watching the man with Napoleon's stature maneuver was like seeing a tank try to speed—painful. "Uh-huh."

"The gossip making the rounds is that she has some crazy notion to hold a beer fundraiser for the veterans' center—and that you're not only helping, but that she's living behind your house."

Mateo kept his mouth shut. He knew a leading statement when he heard one. God knew what Hawson's angle was, but he definitely had one. The man was all about greasing wheels to get his way. Still, he was technically Mateo's boss, since the police chief served at the mayor's prerogative. If the mayor went to the town council asking for his ass on a platter, both cheeks would be delivered within the hour.

"You know no good will come of anything connected to the Sweets—especially Olivia." The mayor practically spit out her name in disgust. "She's not our kind of people. She's all flash and no substance. You and I both know she's not putting on this fundraiser for the good of Salvation's veterans. Imagine going from being famous one day to slinging beer the next. She's going to do whatever it takes to get back in that limelight. I figure a story about a supermodel turned small-town philanthropist would get a lot of eyeballs."

"That's a lot of supposition on your part."

"No, it's a lot of knowledge and expertise. I've been mayor for long enough to know the Sweets inside and out. The whole family is a wreck. Look, we're both Marines. We know what it's like to have a non-hacker in the ranks. The only way to form a cohesive unit is to weed that sucker out. Olivia Sweet is a non-hacker and Salvation is your unit."

Mateo raised his gaze to the photo on the wall above Hawson's left shoulder. It showed his fire team the day before the bombing. Luciana had hung it. He kept meaning to take it down but...

The Sweets were trouble and Olivia wasn't an exception. The town of Salvation, on the other hand, had supported his parents and his sister while he was gone and when he'd had an extended stay at the VA hospital in Richmond. When he'd first come home, there were stilted visits and too cheerful greetings. Those had thankfully stalled out. Now they just left him alone to do his job as police chief. And he liked it that way just fine. They stayed away and he kept them safe. No involvement. No soft spots. No veering from standard operating procedure. He gave the photo one last hard look.

Olivia had been so damned excited as she'd tried to drag him into some sort of fundraiser brainstorming hell at The Kitchen Sink yesterday it had taken everything he had not to join in—something he sure as hell didn't do anymore. "I really don't see the harm in her trying."

"Don't see the harm? Don't you remember the fallout from that so-called coming home documentary she did a few years ago?"

Mateo suppressed his laugh—barely. Hawson had been caught singing to his horse. The video had gone viral and still got airtime occasionally today. The internet never forgets.

"And I'm not just talking about me here. Salvation was the butt of jokes on national TV. People called us the hick's version of heaven. You know the people here. It hurt folks to see their town humiliated. You can't let that happen again."

"And how exactly do you propose I stop that?"

"Keep tabs on her and let me know what she's up to. That's all I'm asking."

"Spy?" That left a dank taste in his mouth.

"That's an ugly word, but yes." Hawson shrugged. "You run the intelligence operation. I'll take care of erecting roadblocks."

"And the veterans' center?" He wasn't about to screw over his brothers. He wouldn't fail them again.

"I'll find the money. The county doesn't have two plug nickels to rub together, but the city has an emergency fund. I can get the town council to agree to make repairs—maybe even rebuild."

That was probably a better deal than any imaginary money Olivia could raise in a fundraiser. Still, he couldn't get onboard with the idea. "I'll think about it."

"What's there to think about? It's either the town you've sworn to protect or Olivia Sweet. Where are your priorities? Where is your loyalty?"

Not with the Sweets. "Right where it belongs." In Salvation.

"Then I can count on you?"

Fuck. If he passed the deal up, he didn't doubt the mayor would hold a grudge no matter how it negatively affected the area's veterans. The little man didn't give a shit about anything except his own power.

"Well, Garcia? Are you in?"

He nodded. "Affirmative."

The mayor stood and reached out his hand. Mateo shook it as briefly as possible. Hawson didn't seem to notice or care. "Good to know that once a Marine, always a Marine still stands. I'll grab that donut and get out of your hair."

As soon as the door clicked shut behind Hawson, the dog relaxed against Mateo's chair. The vibrations from its thick tail thumping against it reverberated up his spine. Without thinking about it, he reached down and scratched the mutt's thick scruff.

"Yeah, I like it best when he leaves too."

The intercom buzzed before Simons's voice sounded. "Hey Chief, don't forget you've got that meeting with Olivia Sweet at the veterans' center in a few."

Of course he did, because his days just kept getting better and better since the model he couldn't stop picturing naked had jumped off a magazine cover and onto Salvation's Main Street.

Twenty minutes early for her meeting with Mateo at the county's wrecked veterans' center, Olivia parked her still mud-caked Fiat in front of the building. She didn't have a plan, but she had a goal and that's all that mattered. Exactly how she'd get Mateo on her side she wasn't sure of yet, but she'd figure out. She always did.

She shielded her eyes against the morning sun and squinted up at the veterans' center. A bright-blue tarp covered most of the gaping hole in the roof, with one corner flapping in the warm spring breeze. Otherwise the rest of the building looks unharmed, if not older than the dirt that made up the sorry excuse for a lawn in front of the squat one-story building.

Okay, this is doable.

How much could it cost to replace a roof? She'd never owned a house or had any home maintenance costs to deal with but surely they could raise the money for a roof during an afternoon beer crawl. Her heels clicked on the cracked sidewalk leading from the street to the front door. She jiggled the knob, opened the door and took a single tentative step inside the abandoned building.

A puff of stale, putrid air slapped her in the face, making her eyes water and her stomach roil. She slapped her hand over her mouth and nose and stumbled back out the door and straight into something hard and immovable that sent a delicious shiver right down her spine.

"Finally coming to your senses and giving up?" Mateo's fingers curled around her elbows, steadying her.

"You showed up." Until that moment, she wasn't sure he would. The fact that he had, made her as nervous as she'd been the first time she'd strutted down the runway in five-inch heels, lingerie and a giant pair of wings. She stepped forward and turned around to face him.

Thank God he wasn't in full uniform or her panties might have melted.

Who was she kidding? The strap of silk covering the good china was already toast just looking at him in his form-fitting jeans and a black polo with the Salvation Police Department logo. The morning sun reflected off his aviator sunglasses, the bottom of which touched the scar twisting its way up the left side of his face.

As if he knew she was looking, he turned his head and stared at the center's leaf-stuffed gutters, blocking her view of that side of his face. "I told you I'd be here."

For somebody who told her the other night to look her fill, he sure didn't like anyone actually doing so. She didn't blame him—staring strangers were never fun—but it pissed her off that he felt the need to hide part of himself.

"And you always keep your word."

That brought his focus back to her. "Always."

Simple and succinct, there was enough cocky self-assurance in that single word to make Olivia realize she needed to regain control of the conversation. The veterans' center. Fundraiser. Hot guy.

No! Not that last one.

She inhaled a deep breath and immediately regretted it. Some of the funk from inside the building clung to her clothes. "I think something died in there."

He poked his head in the center's door and sniffed. "That's urine, not decomposition."

Okay, if she had to pick between the two, she'd go with pee but still... "How can you be sure?"

He took off his sunglasses and quirked an eyebrow. "So are you determined to do this?"

"Yes. Photos will help get people talking." Pulling her phone out of her cross-body purse, she walked to the door.

"Like folks have trouble with that around here." He didn't move from the doorway.

He wasn't completely blocking her entry, but to get in, she'd have to squeeze through the narrow pocket between his biceps and the doorframe. That wasn't gonna happen. She pushed against his arm with one finger, ignoring the electricity that sizzled up her own.

"True, but now they'll be talking about the center and how it needs to be fixed. We'll include the pictures on the fliers for the fundraiser."

Mateo pivoted, giving her just enough space to walk through the door. "Nothing like a little exploitation, huh?"

Her step faltered, but she tamped down her annoyance. The idea was to charm Grumps Garcia into coming over to her side. Telling him to fuck off wouldn't help her cause.

Faking it like the cameras were just around the corner, Olivia turned and gave him her best America's-sexy-sweetheart grin. "Nothing like helping people understand that their help is needed."

It only took three steps inside the center to discover just how much help was needed. Two years of only a poorly secured tarp between the building's interior and Mother Nature hadn't been pretty ones. The hardwood floor was warped from rain that had gotten through the loose tarp and broken windows. Dirt and leaves covered nearly every square inch of the mangled floorboards. Then, there was the stench. Cats, vermin, and God knew what else had used the veterans' center as home base at one time or another, leaving behind now-rotted food scraps and worse.

Olivia squirmed as the urge to get the hell out of there clawed its way up the back of her neck. She may have grown up in the sticks but that didn't mean she'd ever been a fun-loving outdoorsy girl. Dried leaves crunched behind her. Her shoulders jerked up to her earlobes. *Don't let it be a rat. Please don't let it be a rat.*

"You seem a little tense." Mateo was a big guy but if it wasn't for the leaves, she never would have realized he'd left his post by the front door. "More work than you expected?"

A giant "hell yes" to that one. "Not really." He already thought she was in over her head. She wasn't about to confirm it.

She took out her phone and started snapping pictures of the mess while mentally working on the marketing plan. Fliers. Social media. She'd get together with the other craft brewers in the area for the beer crawl, where they'd bring the beer to the customers instead of having people travel from brewery to brewery to sample the latest beers. She could raise money, but could she raise enough to gut the place and start over? Because that's what it was going to take.

Watching her phone screen, she took a step back to get a better shot of the splintered floorboards. Her heel popped through a weak spot in the floor and she stumbled backwards. She flung her arms outward but it was too late. Gravity wasn't about to let her go.

Mateo's strong hands gripped her waist, pulling her back from the brink and up against his hard chest with enough force to nearly knock the breath out of her. At least that was the excuse she was using to explain why she let her cheek rest against his soft cotton shirt for a few beats longer than needed and took an extra-deep inhale of his spicy cologne. It was all medically necessary.

"Thanks."

"No problem." He set her back on her feet but his fingers lingered on her hips.

Not that he had to hold her there. The force keeping her glued to the spot didn't have a damn thing to do with physical touch. It was all about him. He dipped his head lower, his eyes unfocused and hungry. She licked her lips, needing the sensation and anticipating more.

His grip tightened and he froze, inches away from his intended target. "I don't need a model's pity kiss for saving a damsel in distress." His hands dropped back to his side and he took several steps away.

The words, said so low she barely heard him over the blood rushing in her ears, didn't process at first. Then her brain made all the right connections.

"You are such a jackass." Her cheeks pulsed and her heart knocked against her ribs like a felon with a tin cup in a black-and-white jailhouse movie. "I don't pity you. No one needs to pity you because *you've* got that down to a science already."

"If it wasn't pity, then what was it?" He snarled the question.

"Temporary insanity." That still had her in its razor-sharp talons. "You are the last man in the world I'd ever want to kiss."

He strutted over, his boots sending up small clouds of dust as he crossed the center's littered and cracked hardwood floor, stopping half a foot from her. Predatory. Dangerous. Confident. God, the man was her crack and her kryptonite wrapped up together in one muscular package. Her body practically vibrated with need and she parted her tingling lips without meaning to. It just happened.

No. That was a lie. Her right-thinking brain just couldn't keep up with her bad-behaving body.

"The last man you ever want to kiss, huh? Oh honey, we've done a lot more than that." He framed her cheeks with his strong hands and tilted her face up toward him. His hazel eyes darkened to the color of shaded moss as his gaze traveled to her trembling mouth. "Anyway, you're a shitty liar."

God help her, she was, because when he leaned down and kissed her, the last thought she had before her brain turned to mush was: Hell, *yes*.

She fell into the kiss, embracing it with the pent-up need of a woman who'd been denied for an eternity and finally had a peek at heaven. His strong lips teased her, tormented her, tantalized her as desire turned her languid. She wasn't in a hurry to explore this man. She wanted to take her time to rediscover every hard line and rigid plane.

He groaned against her before taking the kiss deeper, seeking out her tongue with his own. It was as if he'd poured gas on a bonfire as her body turned molten. Forget going slow. The all too familiar desire pulsing between her legs gave her other ideas. Needing to touch him, she reached out and glided her palms up his shirt, her fingers finding the buttons and releasing the top two.

Mateo's strong fingers wrapped around her wrist like a vise and he broke the kiss. An air of right-on-the-edge-of-out-of-control wildness surrounded him. His gaze dropped to her kiss-swollen lips and her eyes began to flutter closed.

He brushed his thumb across her bottom lip. "You are nothing but trouble."

If he'd meant it to censure her, then he had the wrong girl. Trouble wasn't a dirty word when you were a Sweet.

"Maybe you need some of that in your life." She drew his thumb into her mouth, swirling her tongue around its tip.

His body went rigid and his eyes darkened with desire but instead of kissing her again, he mumbled something in Spanish under his breath, spun on his heel and strode out of the veterans' center.

Olivia didn't try to stop him. She'd let him think he'd won this skirmish, or at least that it was a draw. Truth be told, she'd gotten under his skin. Tracing her fingertips across her still-tingling lips, she had to admit, he'd gotten under hers as well. And that hadn't been the plan at all. He'd already broken her heart once. She wasn't about to let him stomp it to smithereens again.

Chapter Seven

Silence wasn't just golden, it was all Mateo wanted in the world—especially after he'd spent the past few days ducking Olivia, her tempting-as-hell lips, her flowery-smelling shampoo in his bathroom and her fundraiser plans. She'd left at first light with Luciana. Not that he was keeping track of her movements, it just made sense for him to stay in the know—not because of what that jackass Hawson, but because it made it easier to keep himself on guard.

Now he finally had all the silence he could want, but not for much longer. The soft breeze carried the sound of gravel being crunched under tires in through the open kitchen window. Steaming cup of coffee in one hand and *conches blancas* pastry in the other, he padded across the varnished oak floors to the large bay window overlooking his half-mile-long driveway.

The cabin sat at the peak of a long gravel drive and tall pine trees stood guard on the other three sides. Thanks to Mother Nature and the way sound carried up the hill, no one could get within two miles without him knowing.

The list of people he never wanted darkening his doorstep was a long one, but the man heading his way was near the very top. The mayor's Cadillac barreled toward the house, spitting out gravel from beneath its tires and coming to a stop at the bend in the circular paved parking area big enough for six cars. Mateo finished off the pastry as he watched Hawson, jaw set in a determined line, hustle up to his door. The mayor was a man on a mission.

The pounding on the thick oak front door boomed through the cavernous foyer, echoing through the blessedly empty cabin. Mateo took a sip of coffee and waited. The mayor hammered on the door some more. Someone wasn't going to be avoided today. Wasn't that just his luck? Trouble dogged his feet more than that mangy mutt Luciana had taken off his hands this morning for some adoption event. He set his mug down on the granite kitchen counter. It could be worse. It could be Olivia.

He crossed the foyer in time with a third set of heavy-fisted raps from Salvation's insistent mayor and jerked open the door. Hawson had one hand raised as if about to knock again and a blue piece of paper crumpled in the other.

"Have you seen this?" Hawson shoved the mangled paper in Mateo's direction. "You were supposed to be keeping me updated."

Mateo didn't bother to answer as he took the paper from the mayor's ham-fisted grip. Creased and beat up as it was, there was still no missing the message.

HELP RAISE A GLASS FOR THE SALVATION VETERANS' CENTER AT THE SWEET SALVATION BREWERY – ALL PROCEEDS GO TOWARD REBUILDING THE CENTER. VOLUNTEERS, EXHIBITORS AND DONATIONS NEEDED! SIGN UP TODAY.

Part of him couldn't help but be impressed. While he'd been doing everything he could to dodge her, she'd been working her hot little ass off. There just might be more to Olivia Sweet than what looked good on a magazine cover.

He neatly folded the fundraiser flyer in half and handed it back to the mayor. "I told you I'd keep an eye on her. I did. She's not doing anything crazy."

Hawson sputtered for a minute before any actual words came out. "She will. Believe you me, before this is over, the whole thing will be about her." He balled up the flyer in his hand and winged it across the porch. The blue paper rolled to a stop in the corner, the only touch of bright color in the otherwise pristine gray stone porch. "She'll use this as a springboard for her sorry-ass excuse of a career as a D-list celebrity. I thought you were on Salvation's side. You have to stop it."

Only years of Marine-conditioned discipline kept Mateo from scooping up the mayor and tossing him off the porch. The smart thing was to go along with the mayor's scheme. What did he care about Olivia's plans as long as the veterans' center was rebuilt like Hawson had promised? She was a thorn he'd shoved into his side to remind him of everything he couldn't have anymore.

"And how do you propose I stop her?"

"Any means necessary," the mayor said.

He glanced over at the bright-blue paper ball sitting in the corner and then back at the Napoleon wannabe plotting his little sabotage on Mateo's front porch. He'd always hated bullies. He'd agreed to keep an eye on Olivia's activities, not sabotage the fundraiser.

"No."

Hawson's eyebrows shot up and the vein in his temple puffed out. "What do you mean, no?"

"Do I need to go grab a dictionary?"

"I thought you were a man, *a Marine*, that I could depend on." Hawson delivered the insult with the flair of a carnival sideshow barker.

It had about the same effect on Mateo as the last time someone tried to get him to play one of those crooked games at the county fair. "Seems you were wrong."

"From the stories I've heard about your last deployment, I'm not the only one. Thought you would have learned the danger of disregarding an order."

Fire of shame and guilt ate its way up from his gut as fast and hot as the roadside explosion that had killed the rest of his four-Marine fire team in Afghanistan. "Get off my property before I dropkick your ass to the highway."

Hawson puffed up like a posturing goose. "Don't you threaten me, boy, unless you want to be out of a job."

Mateo laughed and leaned against the doorframe. "I don't make threats, just deliver on promises."

The mayor's round cheeks went crimson and his eyes bulged. If he didn't calm the fuck down, he was going to have a heart attack on the front porch, and there was no way Mateo would be giving the asshole mouth to mouth.

Just when he thought his day couldn't get any worse, Olivia's ridiculous yellow Fiat sped up the driveway, kicking out gravel, followed by Luciana's minivan. Some pop diva blared from the Fiat's speakers and out of the open windows just barely louder than Olivia's off-tune singing and the happy yaps of that damned mutt, both of whom were about as welcome during his breakfast as a cardboard-tasting veggie omelet in an MRE. He didn't know when his place had turned into grand fucking central but it had.

Luciana and Olivia got out of their cars and that ugly excuse for a dog sprinted past them both, bounded up the stairs and sat down on Mateo's right shoe.

"I see how it is." The mayor's beady eyes narrowed and he zeroed in on Olivia as she began to saunter toward them. "Good to know what kind of foxhole you're really interested in."

Even though his muscles twitched with the need to smack the smug look off the mayor's face, Mateo took a deliberate step back so he wouldn't be in striking distance. "You have five seconds."

Hawson opened his mouth, but clamped it right back shut before any more bile could come out. He spun on his heel and clomped down the front steps, giving Olivia and Luciana a wide berth on the stairs before getting into his Cadillac and hightailing it off Burnett's Hill.

In a perfect world, the dictatorial mayor would never darken his doorstep again, but Mateo had seen too much of the imperfect to ever believe that would happen—especially not when the personification of trouble stood not three feet away in a short skirt and sky-high heels.

Per usual, Luciana had taken over his kitchen, unloading groceries he hadn't asked her to buy and stuffing homemade enchiladas in the fridge that he hadn't asked her to make. Ever since he'd gotten out of the hospital, she'd made these weekly trips out to the cabin like he couldn't fend for himself when she knew damn well he could microwave like nobody's business.

"Would it kill you to buy some fresh fruit instead of stocking up on protein drinks and frozen food?" Luciana shut the refrigerator door with a disgusted snort. "So what did His Highness want?"

"The usual." If being a pain in the butt counted as the usual, which, with Tyrell Hawson, it did.

"You have a 'usual' with the mayor?" Olivia plopped one last fresh flower into the vase she'd brought with her from the car and stood back to admire the totally unnecessary colorful bouquet taking up residence on the oversized island in his otherwise stark, mostly stainless-steel kitchen.

She glanced up at him with a satisfied smile on her face that knocked the air out of his lungs. It was the kind of look that had made men throughout history start wars and conquer new territory just to impress a woman. Some men, but not him. He didn't have room in his life for grocery-store flowers and women so beautiful it made his scars ache—no matter how good she felt in his arms or just how badly he wanted to touch her every damn time he saw her.

Clamping his teeth together, he shoved the wisp of possibility out of his mind and turned on his heel, nearly going down in a heap because of the constantly underfoot dog.

"So what's with the mutt?" The canine's tail thumped against his calf. "I thought he was getting adopted today."

Luciana shrugged. "Ellen from The Kitchen Sink came by with a box of puppies. You know those cuties were going to go first."

She immediately turned and squashed the plastic grocery bags into a ball and stuffed them in the recycling bin she'd brought on a previous visit. But Mateo wasn't fooled. He knew how his sister worked. If he didn't act quick, he was going to end up with the furry mutt forever.

"That doesn't answer my question. Why is the dog here?"

"He sure does like you." Olivia circled around the island and squatted down near his feet, nuzzling her cheek against the dog's scruff.

Just the brush of Olivia's bare shoulder against his hip sent his thoughts veering away from the problem at hand and to the feel of her silky skin faster than a Hellfire missile.

Get a grip, Garcia. He took a step back. The dog followed, but Olivia—thankfully—did not. He looked up at the custom tin ceiling and shoved his hands deep into his shorts pockets to keep from reaching out for her. When he dropped his gaze, his sister was looking right at him with a knowing smirk on her face that made his scar itch.

His sister had many faults, but being unobservant wasn't one of them. She looked from him to the dog to Olivia and back again. If she got any crazy ideas, his life would go from peaceful to a shitstorm in a nanosecond and there wouldn't be a damn thing he could do about it.

"Luciana." He'd used that tone a thousand times on fresh recruits and seasoned Marines alike. With them it had gotten immediate results. With his sister, all it got him was a well-practiced eye roll.

She gave him an innocent smile that would have fooled anyone not blood-related. "It's only until we find this little doggie a home."

Oh no. His house—shit, his *life* wasn't made to be shared. "I'm not a dog person. I'm not a cat person. I'm not even a people person."

"Really?" Luciana rounded on him. "That is total news to everyone here. Maybe it's time you got out of your comfort zone, stopped hiding in your own little private fortress and opened yourself up to new experiences."

"I'm not hiding." He looked at Olivia. "Anyway, I'm already helping with the fundraiser."

"Speaking of which," Olivia said. "We had an idea."

With Olivia on his right and his sister on his left, Mateo was trapped. "I'm not going to like this."

"Probably not." Luciana grinned. "But you'll get over that."

"We want you to sing at the fundraiser," Olivia said.

His blood went cold.

He used to sing all the time—so much so that his nickname in his unit had been Mic. It killed time between missions and broke up the monotony of life on a forward operating base in the middle of a country half a world away from home and everything familiar. Old Motown songs, those had been his specialty. But the last time he'd sung a note had been a week before the explosion that had torn the guys he'd fought with to shreds. He didn't have to close his eyes to see the devastation his own mistake had caused; it was always with him—awake, asleep or in-between.

"I don't sing anymore."

"Why not?" Olivia asked.

Because he didn't think he could hit the notes anymore. His singing voice, like everything else, had gotten shredded in the IED explosion. Luciana was wrong. He wasn't hiding from the people in Salvation; he was protecting them from seeing what kind of man one of their own had become. But he wasn't about to say that out loud.

"Have you seen me?" He gestured to the twisted mess that used to be the left side of his face. "Nobody wants to look at this under a spotlight."

Olivia moved in close, her fingers brushing across the map of scars on his face before dropping her hand to her side. "You care a lot more about your scars than anyone else in town does."

It was the first time anyone without medical initials after their name had touched his face.

Unable to process his reaction to that, he fell back on his best weapon: anger. "That's rich, coming from someone who doesn't just look like a model but used to be one."

Her face smoothed out into a beautiful mask of imperviousness. "That was low."

That's where he'd aimed, and he always hit his target. Maybe if he did more of that, everyone would finally leave him the fuck alone.

"I'm sick and tired of everyone coming around trying to get me to do what they want," he bellowed. "Hawson wants what he wants. You two want me to work on this fundraiser and sing in front of half the town—of course, that's if anyone shows up to this thing. Wait. I take that back. Oh, they'll show. If for no other reason than because the people in this town love to watch a train wreck."

Olivia's cheeks blazed and she sucked in a deep breath, but she held her ground when a lot of others would have gone running. "You're a real asshole, Mateo Garcia."

"Glad you noticed." He grabbed his coffee mug from the counter and took a sip of the now-cold liquid. "Now, if you two don't mind, I have things to do."

"Come on, Olivia," Luciana said. "Let's get out of here."

The two women got as far as the front door before he realized they'd left something behind. "You forgot your dog."

"No we didn't," Olivia snapped. "Maybe it's time for you to start remembering that there's more to life than that massive chip you have welded to your shoulder."

They were out the door before he could come up with a scathing comeback.

The dog gave a forlorn half howl, snagging Mateo's attention. "You want to go with them? Good. Go."

He hustled out the door, the dog close on his heels, but he wasn't quick enough to catch Luciana before her minivan was halfway down the drive. Olivia was nowhere to be seen—no doubt she'd stormed off to her cabin.

Mateo stood on the front porch as the dog whined and nudged his leg.

"What the hell do you want?"

The dog whimpered, pulling at the few heartstrings Mateo had left. Now he was scaring a homeless dog. Shit. He really *had* turned into an asshole. He hunkered down on the top step. The dog must have taken it as an invitation because he crawled into his lap and shivered.

"Shhh, boy." He leaned back to make his lap bigger and rubbed up and down the dog's spine.

Still the mutt whimpered.

Mateo didn't mean to sing. The notes just came out as he petted the dog's newly washed fur.

"Sitting on the dock of the bay, watching the tide roll away." The sound was rough and rusty, the notes broken in places where they shouldn't be and sharp as a KA-BAR knife in others. Still, he sang to the shivering dog in his lap until the mutt relaxed...and for a good long time after his snores began.

Chapter Eight

Even the tallest shoes in Olivia's still-unpacked suitcase weren't going to make this day any better. The first annual Sweet Salvation Brewery Veterans' Fundraiser volunteer informational meeting had disaster written all over it. With only a few minutes to go before it was set to kick off, Olivia had everything in place—except the volunteers.

"Just the little things," Olivia mumbled to herself while glaring up at the fast-darkening sky as storm clouds rolled in from the West. *Oh yeah, feel free to pile it on, Mother Nature.*

For the fifth time, she double-checked the tables to ensure each had a donation jar fashioned out of a beer growler to take back to town and set up at local businesses to collect donations; a stack of flyers featuring photos showing the damage to the center to post on church bulletin boards and at community gathering spots; and plenty of pens in case someone wanted to write a ginormous six-figure check. Wouldn't that be nice? One fundraising volunteer meeting and they'd raise enough to fix the center and get the Sweet family into Salvation's good graces months before her new niece or nephew arrived. Now that would be a win-win situation.

A fat drop of rain hit Olivia square in the middle of her forehead then rolled down the bridge of her nose before dripping off the tip. Lightning flashed in the distance. One. Two. Three. Four. Five. Six. *Bang*. There went the thunder.

Miranda rushed over, armed with an empty crate that would normally be filled with freshly bottled beer. "Looks like we're moving this shindig indoors, unless you put a last-minute wet T-shirt contest on the schedule of events."

That made Olivia laugh. "Maybe next year."

Moving fast to dodge the ever-increasing raindrops, she and Miranda worked together to get all of the decorations inside to the tasting room as the thunder came sooner and sooner after the lightning bolts that lit up the sky. They carried in the last dripping crate load just as the skies opened up and dumped enough water to limit the visibility to a few feet outside the brewery's front door.

Her stomach sank.

Miranda came and stood on her right side and Natalie on her left. They stood there like sentries watching the rain come down.

"I'm sure it'll pass," Miranda said, sounding about as convincing as a sinner begging for entry at the pearly gates. "People will come to volunteer."

Okay. This sucked, but it could still work. The tasting room was set up for a good-sized crowd and she'd arranged it so it would look as it would for the fundraiser in two weeks. There was a stage at one end for the band and they could run the blind beer-tasting challenge from the large bar in the back corner. People cold line up, taste the beer and deposit their vote for best beer in a comment box at the end of the bar. That was if the other breweries agreed to participate in the fundraiser. "Any word from the other breweries about participating?"

Natalie shook her head. "Nada."

She glanced over at the clock. Fifteen minutes until go time.

Olivia bit the inside of her cheek to keep herself from groaning out loud. She was used to shit going south fast—what Sweet wasn't?—but this was ridiculous. "Too many coincidences for me."

"Yep." Miranda nodded. "I think someone is trying to submarine the fundraiser before we even get a chance to train volunteers."

It would't be the first time. The Sweets hadn't exactly been welcome in Salvation since...oh, since the town had been founded. Cattle thieves. Moonshiners. Rabble-rousers. The family was guilty on all counts. But Olivia and her sisters had been on the up and up since birth. Well, her sisters had been. Olivia had embraced the Sweet family crazy.

"Who would do it?" Natalie asked.

"Isn't that the million-dollar question?" The list was long—with Mateo and his "usual" with the uptight Salvation mayor right at the top of it. He hadn't been shy about his opposition to the fundraiser even after he'd agreed to help. Add that to the blowup last week and he made for a decent suspect.

"We need to cancel." She sank down into the closest chair, wishing she could sink below the floorboards. So much for her grand plan.

"Don't cancel. Postpone." Natalie grabbed her clipboard from behind the bar and hustled over to the table where Olivia sat contemplating her latest failure. "Call it a rainout and say that you'll reschedule the volunteer training."

As far as believable excuses went, it made sense. Still, the abject failure of the day had her trigger shy.

"What makes you think anyone will show up next time?"

"Because you won't give them a choice." Miranda sat down beside them. "You busted your hump to get something put together in two weeks. Imagine what you could do with a couple more?"

If she could turn the fundraiser into the event of the year in Salvation, there was no way the people in town could stay away. She just had to give them something they couldn't get anywhere else. She needed to use her Sweet-inherited flair for the extreme for good and everything would work out.

"I could call in some favors from my friends in Harbor City, get some great raffle prizes." Her modeling days had left her with a phone filled with contact information for some of the coolest photographers, artists and creative types in the industry. "Maybe Steffano would agree to do a makeover in between his styling gigs."

Natalie began forming a list of possible giveaways on her clipboard. "See, this is a good thing."

It was, but Olivia couldn't shake the itchy feeling at the back of her neck that something more than freaky coincidence had happened to sink the fundraiser, and she was going to find out exactly what—or who—it was.

Olivia pushed open the front door of The Kitchen Sink. The diner was packed, extinguishing her last flicker of hope that aliens had kidnapped every single citizen of Salvation and thus explaining why no one had showed for the volunteer meeting.

Ruby Sue looked up from her perch on a stool behind the cash register. "Oh good, you brought me one of those growly things."

"Are you sure you don't mind putting this up here?" She put the wide-mouth growler down by the register, next to the sign warning those with bad attitudes would be charged a pain-in-the-butt fee.

"What fool would have a problem collecting change for a good cause?"

"Every other person in Salvation." What had she been thinking, trying to throw a fundraiser that would get the town to stop crossing the street to avoid rubbing elbows with the Sweets? Maybe Mateo was right. Maybe this was more than she could do.

"Volunteer meeting didn't go so well, huh?" Ruby Sue asked, but the sympathetic look on her face said she knew the answer to that.

"It didn't go at all. No one showed up." Failure formed a lead weight in her stomach.

Ruby Sue shook her head. "Idiots."

"That's one word for them." She pinched her lips together before she gave the dozen or so other words that would fit the close-minded, gossiping, grudge-holding people in her hometown.

It would be one thing if she or her sisters had ever actually done anything to raise the town's hackles, but it had been like this for as long as Olivia could remember. She and her sisters had been born in the backseat of her parents' Chevrolet parked in front of the Stop and Sip. Salvation's citizens had taken that as proof that this generation of Sweets was just as trashy as the moonshine runners, naked protestors and possible DMV arsonists who'd come before. The whole situation sucked.

A couple approached the register, bill in hand, and Olivia made her way over to the pie case. Two pieces of pecan pie were left. Finally, something was going right. One for her and one to bribe some information out of Mateo. She'd bet her designer stilettos that he knew who the head of the snake was, and just how she could chop off its head.

"Hey, Ellen." She smiled at the waitress beside the pie case. "Can I get these two to go?"

"Sure," she said. "Just let me take a couple of sweet teas out to table four and then I'll get them wrapped up for you."

"Thanks." She settled down on the stool and took out her wallet. Her last ten dollar bill until her first Sweet Salvation Brewery paycheck came in tomorrow, but the pie was a necessary expense.

"Hope you're not planning to snarf down both of those," an all too familiar voice said from behind her. "You know how the camera puts on ten pounds."

Turning, she faced Salvation's mayor and number one Sweet family hater, Tyrell Hawson. "Thanks for the advice."

"Just trying to be helpful." He curled his lips back in what he probably thought of as a smile. "Maybe you can help me out now."

She leveled a hard stare at him and raised one eyebrow. "How's that?"

"Forget your fundraiser, go back to L.A. and take your sisters with you." He said it all with the soft, good-natured delivery of a guy just trying to do her a solid.

His words sank in, each one slicing open the wounds from childhood. The parents who didn't want their kids playing with those Sweet girls. The whispers. The stares. The hell of growing up a Sweet in Salvation. She'd never understood how someone could think they knew everything about her and her sisters just because of their last name.

"Why do you hate us so much?" She didn't mean to ask, and God knew Tyrell was the last person she should have shown even the slightest bit of weakness.

He narrowed his eyes and every bit of fake good ol' boy vanished from his round face. "Because this is a good town—an honest, God-fearing town filled with hardworking people—and we don't need your kind around here."

"What kind is that?" Anger flooded her veins, burning with decades of frustration. She stood up, towering over the shorter mayor and enjoying how he shrank back. "Someone like Miranda, a business genius who brought back the Sweet Salvation Brewery from the edge of disaster and saved the jobs of dozens of people in Salvation? Someone like Natalie, who could make efficiency more efficient and gave up a thriving business to grow a local company? No, it can't be them, so it must be me. I'm just a retired model who was on the cover of a dozen magazines."

"But those days are long gone for you, aren't they girlie?" he snarled. "Now you're just a porn star."

Her heart stuttered to a stop before starting again with a frantic rush that sent her pulse pounding through her body.

He couldn't know. There was no way. Her name hadn't been attached to the photos her ex had posted. There'd been speculation and gossip, but no confirmation. It had been the one positive of the whole Larry shitstorm, but it sounded like her ex had gone and revealed that it was her.

Tyrell puffed up his chest and leered at her tits. “Oh yeah, the town is going crazy this afternoon about the naked pictures of you all over the internet. Some tabloid TV show broke the story today. What a slut bimbo move on your part. What did you think would happen when you took those kinds of pictures?”

That she was sharing something with the man she’d thought she loved. That he’d never break her trust by sharing the pictures. That the last thing Larry would ever do was share the photos on a revenge-porn site. Yeah, she may have been naïve, but she hadn’t done a damn thing wrong, and she sure didn’t deserve to be called a bimbo slut by a jerk like Tyrell.

“You bastard.”

His face turned six shades of red and a sheen of sweat glistened on his forehead. “If anyone’s paternity should be questioned, it would be that baby your sister is carrying.”

She lifted her hand lightning fast and swung it with furious speed. Her palm cracked against the mayor’s chubby cheek, sending him reeling back.

“Now that’s a Sweet for you,” he snarled, one hand pressed to the palm print on his face.

White-hot fury zipped through Olivia and she jabbed a finger hard into his shoulder. “You *ever* talk about my family like that again and I will do a helluva lot worse than slapping your sorry ass.”

“A publicly expressed direct threat.” Triumph lifted his volume and his mouth curled in a smug smile, probably the most sincere one he’d ever had. “I have witnesses.”

Olivia looked up. Everyone in The Kitchen Sink was staring at her, some with mouths agape and others with I-knew-this-would-happen looks of barely restrained superiority.

Fuck. She knew better than to take the bait—but she had. Inhaling a deep breath, she turned on her heel to face the pie case and regain her bearings.

Ellen, her eyes round, pushed a white to-go bag across the counter to Olivia. "Your pie."

If it had been anything else but Ruby Sue's pecan pie, the temptation to say to hell with the consequences and use the bag to whack the pompous mayor over the head might have been too strong to deny. There was more on the line than just her anger though. She had to find a way to make Salvation accept her family, or her niece or nephew would be sentenced to the same sad childhood she'd had.

Still, she couldn't deny it soothed her a little to see Hawson flinch when she grabbed the bag off the counter and took a step toward him before turning and walking out of The Kitchen Sink.

Mateo popped open a beer and carried it to the couch, where he sat down and rested his bare feet on the coffee table. The baseball game was already in the second inning on the big screen that dominated the living room, the dog was asleep under the coffee table, snoring louder than the thunderstorm earlier that day, and the Yankees had just scored.

It was as close to heaven as he usually got, but a restlessness made his toes itch. The crack of a baseball bat hitting one out of the park followed by the crowd's cheers blasted out of his sound bar, filling the large living room up to the cathedral ceiling.

He downed the beer in a series of long gulps and padded into the kitchen for another. Too many of his buddies had come home only to get lost in a bottle, so his rule was one and done, but a couple of drinks was the only thing that numbed the fidgety need to move that had taken up residence since she'd come back.

Olivia Sweet.

He should have known he was doomed the night she'd half slid down that muddy drive in time to watch him pull her car out of the muck. She'd stood there in rain boots and yoga pants that clung to her ass for dear life and declared she wasn't going anywhere. Since then, if she wasn't dogging his steps, she was haunting his nights or making his bathroom smell like wildflowers and strawberries. He couldn't shake her—real and dressed or imagined and naked.

Sliding his hand beneath the elastic waist of his basketball shorts, he curled it around his half-hard cock and wondered what it would be like if he actually touched her like he used to. She had melted in his arms in the veterans' center. Her skin had been so soft and her mouth so willing... God, the damage they could do to each other with enough time and condoms. He brought his hand up and down the shaft, picturing the curve of her neck and the creamy flesh of her tits that had been visible above her shirt's neckline. How many times had he jerked off to her three *Sports Illustrated* covers, remembering how she'd felt underneath him? Too many to count, and he was about to add another without even the aid of seeing a picture of her in the world's tiniest white bikini.

Just as he got a good rhythm going, the dog barked and scrambled out from underneath the coffee table as if he'd been goosed by a fireplace poker. A second later, the sound of a car making its way up the driveway filtered in through the open kitchen windows. Cock at half mast and wearing only his basketball shorts, he wasn't exactly ready for visitors. Not that he ever was. Hand still holding position, he watched the vehicle approach until the security lights near the parking pad illuminated Olivia's yellow Fiat. His cock jumped in anticipation.

The dog whined and pawed the front door.

Mateo gave his hands a quick rinse in the kitchen sink before making his way over to the door, walking more bowlegged than normal. He glanced through the window. Instead of walking around back to the cabin, she was heading right for his front door.

Grabbing the newspaper off the entry table, he closed the distance to the door and positioned the newspaper in front of his loose basketball shorts. It wasn't the greatest boner camouflage but it was better than opening his door with a flag pole in his pants.

Putting on his best leave-me-alone snarl, even though everything below the waist was happy as hell to see Olivia, he jerked open the door. "What do you want?"

Seemingly undeterred by his less-than-cheerful greeting, she marched up the stairs, her hips swaying with each forward step. "Hello to you to."

"That doesn't answer the question." He eyeballed the paper bag in one hand and a growler of beer from Sweet Salvation Brewery in the other. Armed with goodies and wearing a bright-blue tank, a filmy floral skirt and a honey-I'm-home smile, she looked as if she'd expected the warmest of welcomes. Maybe she'd hit her head at the fundraiser volunteer meeting this afternoon before they'd called the whole thing off.

"My God, you are prickly. If after the day I've had, *I* can still be almost civil, then so can you." Not that it seemed to bother her one iota.

"What happened to you, break a nail?"

"I wish." She sighed and her shoulders slumped. "My scumbag ex posted private pictures of me to a revenge-porn site and now some shitty tabloid TV show got wind of them and is sharing them with the world—including the entire population of Salvation, which is gossiping about that trashy Sweet triplet as we speak."

A tidal wave of white-hot rage rushed through him. No one deserved to have that happen to them. It was a violation and it was wrong, but it wasn't always illegal. "You're not trashy and your ex is a real asshole."

"Nothing I can do about it now, so I've brought comfort food." She held out the bag, showcasing The Kitchen Sink's logo on one side. "I brought two slices of Ruby Sue's pecan pie, but if you don't want one of them, I guess I could share it with the dog."

She plopped down on his porch, her skirt fluttering down to rest midway up her toned thighs, and took out an individually wrapped slice. Inhaling deeply, she closed her eyes and made some sort of sound that made him think of all the things he could do to her to get her to make it again.

The dog, traitor that he was, happily did the waggle-butt dance over to her side.

People had ended up with black eyes in mad scrambles for the last piece of Ruby Sue's pie. Letting a dog slurp it up was like Photoshopping his ugly mug onto a Victoria's Secret model. He couldn't let that happen.

"You're not really going to give that to the dog." Just saying the words was like getting a sharp jab to the sternum.

Olivia looked up and the security light picked up every blonde highlight in her hair, giving her a halo when he knew damn well that woman had horns. "Why not?" She batted her eyelashes at him. "It wouldn't hurt the cute little doggie."

The animal in question was in some sort of blissful nirvana state sitting hip-to-hip next to Olivia. His eyes were closed and his nose was going a mile a minute.

"But it's Ruby Sue's pie." He could practically taste the sugary sweetness on his tongue. "You can't waste that on the dog."

Olivia flipped her hair over one nearly bare shoulder dusted with freckles. "So invite me in."

Now that way lay trouble. "What are you, a vampire that needs an invitation?"

"Worse. I'm a Sweet." She gave him an exaggerated wink. "But a big tough guy like you couldn't be afraid of having little ol' me in your house, could you?"

Want slammed through him with the power of a fifty-caliber rifle. Every taunt that came out of her beyond- kissable pink mouth was a promise that couldn't be fulfilled, but damn if it wasn't the only thing he could think about.

Olivia couldn't believe she'd actually made it through the front door without busting into frustrated tears or going on a rant about what had just gone down at The Kitchen Sink. Finally today, something was going according to plan. Now if she could just work this right, she'd actually get Mateo to help with the fundraiser that the mayor was trying so damn hard to ruin.

And if she could manage to keep her attention on her goal instead of Mateo's cute butt, she might actually get what she needed.

She followed Mateo into his gourmet kitchen that would have looked right at home in *Architectural Digest*. Large windows spanned both walls, giving anyone inside a front-row seat to the natural beauty of Burnett's Hill. In contrast with the warm woods and greenery outside, everything inside was cold and modern—stainless-steel appliances, black granite countertops and dark, nearly black cherry-wood cabinets filled the large space. Strong, intimidating and immense, just like the man who stood on one side of the large kitchen island eyeing her warily.

He should be wary. She'd brought her A game tonight. After what had gone down with the mayor, she didn't have a choice. The fundraiser had to be a success.

Setting the sixty-four-ounce growler filled with the brewery's latest craft brew and the pie on the island, Olivia walked to the cabinets beside the refrigerator. "Where are your glasses?"

"Why?"

She opened one cabinet—plates—and then another. Jackpot. "For the beer." She grabbed two tall glasses, spun on her heel and strolled back to the island, where she unscrewed the growler top and poured.

“I don’t like beer.” His gaze was zeroed in on the glass of Sweet Salvation Brewery’s latest amber ale as he leaned against the counter, arms folded over his bare chest.

Up until now, she’d done a pretty good job of keeping her focus on Mateo’s face, which was distracting enough, and not the miles of sinewy muscle crisscrossing his torso. But once her line of vision dipped down, there was no coming back up. It was like drowning in hotness.

Tattoos of four military helmets formed a band around one thick biceps, one of several tattoos that decorated his broad chest so thick with muscle he could give the male fitness models she knew a run for their money. The elastic waistband of his shorts hung low on his waist, giving her a full view of his six-pack abs. If only he’d tug them down just a little bit lower, she could see almost all of the muscles forming a V at his hips—or at least that’s what she imagined. If she actually saw them, she’d probably pass out. Hell, she was feeling a little woozy as it was.

Pull it together, Olive Breath. You’ve seen plenty of men totally naked.

Problem was, none of them made her stomach flutter like Mateo.

Focus!

Sucking in a deep breath, she tore her gaze away from him and to the recycling bin next to her at the end of the island.

“You don’t like beer?” She nudged his open-top bin with her toe and the telltale rattle of glass bottles sounded. “Really?”

He cleared his throat. “I make exceptions every once in a while.”

She held out a glass to him. “So make one now.”

Their fingers grazed as he took the glass from her and electricity shot up her arm and gave everything from the neck down the fizzy, unsettled feeling of an itch that needed to be scratched. She wasn't sure when but sometime between walking in the front door and pouring the beer, she'd lost control of the situation and she needed to get it back.

He took a long, slow sip of beer, the whole time watching her over the top of his glass with the steady glare of a born skeptic. "What is it you're after?"

When she'd pulled up in her car? His help. Now? Getting a peek—and more—at what was underneath his basketball shorts.

"A few minutes of relaxation to sip good beer." She dipped one finger into the foam at the top of her beer, gathered just enough of it then sucked it off the tip.

His heated gaze went straight to her mouth and his jaw tightened. For someone so intent on denying the attraction, it was definitely there—no doubt about it. The air thickened around them and desire pooled in her belly. With deliberate slowness, she licked the last drops off the center of her bottom lip.

He set his glass down on the counter with a clank that echoed in the quiet kitchen.

A few years ago they'd be fucking by now—against the refrigerator, bent over the island, flat on the floor with her riding him hard and fast. Denial had never been their thing. Now it felt as though it was all they had in common anymore.

"And then a few more to drown my shitty day in Ruby Sue's pecan pie." She leaned forward to grab one of the forks he'd placed on the oversized island. Inhaling a deep breath, she sank a fork into the pie, lifted the bite and held it out to him. "Want some?"

He gulped, lust as plain on his face as the scars he used as an excuse to keep people at a distance—but he didn't move to take the bite she'd offered. "You're not playing fair."

The accusation, true as it may be, delivered in his rough bass sent a shiver down her spine. "Who said I was playing?" Shrugging, she turned the fork and ate the bite of pie herself.

Fuck. It really was good. Not exactly what she was hungry for right now, but it was beginning to look like a sugar rush was the only kind of satisfaction she was going to get. *What a shame.*

"Why don't you just spit out what it is you're after and save us the charade," he demanded. "We both know I'm not anyone's idea of good company."

"And whose fault is that?" She tossed the fork down and it skittered across the island. "As someone who has spent her life being shunned by the people of Salvation, let me tell you that being a hated outcast isn't as fun you seem to think. Get rid of that giant chip on your shoulder and you might realize that."

Something dark flashed across his face and her breath stalled in her lungs. Then, as if someone had flipped a switch, he smirked and gave her the slow up and down. It was the kind of look he'd given her a million times after spotting her at a hotel bar or in elevator when she was coming to meet him. Dangerous. All-knowing. Totally trouble. Without giving her time to reorient herself to the new order of things, he stalked around the island, stopping beside her.

He didn't touch her. He didn't have to. She was lost to the heat and the need and the hunger sweeping through her.

"If I'm hiding some heart of gold under this beastly exterior, then what are you hiding, Olivia?" He traced his fingertip down the length of her neck, following the erratic beat of her jugular vein.

His touch was too hot, too good, too much. She thought she'd known the rules of this game, but she was wrong.

Mentally reeling, she grabbed ahold of the one thing that had nothing to do with how her body was reacting to his—the truth. "I know the mayor is trying to ruin any chance we have of holding a successful fundraiser for the veterans' center. I want to know what I have to do to get the town to see what an idiot he is." Her heart hammered against her ribs and her thighs trembled. "I need you."

His help. His touch. Him.

Mateo turned his head, bringing their lips close. "Then you're in trouble."

For a heartbeat she didn't move, didn't breath, didn't think.

Then his lips touched hers, and all she could do was fall into the kiss.

Chapter Nine

Touching Olivia was like coming home whole, instead of with his head wrapped in bandages and on enough pain medications to knock a bull to its knees.

Except unlike during that hellish flight from the base in Germany, where they'd stabilized his condition enough for the return stateside, standing in his kitchen with his arms wrapped around Olivia, he knew everything wasn't going to be all right. Still, he couldn't stop himself from wanting to believe it would be. And that hope? It was even more dangerous than the feel of her fingers on his chest or the taste of pecan pie on her lips.

Not wanting to but knowing he didn't have a choice, he pulled back for a breath before he lost himself and took things too far. He was supposed to scare her off with his touch—make her run away to the safety of her cabin and leave him in peace. Instead, she was electricity under his skin, unpredictable and wild.

He fisted his hands at his sides before he reached for her again. "Being this close to you and not being able to touch you was supposed to be my penance."

She looked up at him, her cheeks flushed pink and a genuine desire burning in her blue eyes. "For what?"

"Everything." It was the simplest explanation for the wrongs he'd committed and the men who'd died as a result, but the single word cut him deep.

Cupping his face in her palms without even the slightest flinch at touching the eerily smooth scar tissue crisscrossing the left side of his head, she raised herself up to her tiptoes and brushed a kiss across his forehead. "Maybe it's time to stop punishing yourself for past sins."

He wished it was that easy, but it wasn't. So if he was already this deep in, what was one more transgression? Snagging the hem of her tank top between two fingers, he tugged it taut. "I suppose you think you're the woman to show me the way?"

Leaning in close, she whispered into his good ear, "No one knows more about sinning than a Sweet."

"That's what you think." He lifted the hem of her shirt, inching it higher as slowly as he could without losing what was left of his mind. "I'm going show you a thing or two tonight."

She exhaled a shaky breath and took a step back. "Big talk."

"You know I always keep my word." He pulled her shirt over her head and tossed it to the floor.

If he could have turned away from her, he'd crossed that point. There was no going back now. His balls tightened at the sight of the high curve of her tits pushing against the yellow lace of her bra. The material gave just enough of a glimpse of her dusky pink nipples beneath to make pre-come wet the tip of his dick.

"I'm going to fuck you long and hard right here in this kitchen." He skimmed his hands down her sides, dipping in at her waist and flaring out at her generous hips, relishing the way her breath hitched as he made the downward journey. He slipped his hand under her skirt and stopped as soon as his fingers brushed the lace of her thong. "But first I'm going to lay you across this island, spread these long legs as wide as they'll go and feast on that pussy of yours because you're wet for me already, aren't you, honey?"

"Why don't you feel for yourself?" she challenged, her breathy tone showing just how much she hoped he'd pick up the gauntlet she'd thrown.

Like there was any chance of leaving it where it lay. "Trust me. I plan to."

He cupped her ass, lifting her up until her damp center pressed against his dick still tucked away in his basketball shorts but fighting to be free. The urge to yank them down, pull her panties to the side and drive straight and hard into her nearly squeezed the air out of his lungs. Something primitive inside him demanded release to claim her, make her his.

Her tits jiggled against his bare chest when he sat her down on the island and shoved her skirt up to her waist. "Spread your legs."

"Yes, sir." She winked as she stretched out her legs, but an excited flush had spread across her chest—neither of them were playing games anymore.

The center of her delicate yellow thong was several shades darker than the rest and he breathed in the intoxicating scent of her arousal as he slid his thumb across the dewy material. It was heaven and hell in one tiny patch of lace. Ever impatient, she pushed her hips higher, pressing against his thumb.

He gave her covered pussy a playful smack and then rubbed the sensitized spot. "Not yet. I want to hear you moan and beg to come all over my mouth." He pulled the soaked material to the side, revealing her bare pussy lips, puffy and soft with want. "Some things take time."

"Just lick me already," she half begged, half demanded.

"I never said I'd lick you." He ran the backs of his knuckle across her exposed wet folds. "I'm going to feast on you." He released her thong so it covered her up, grasped the thin piece of lace crossing her hip in both hands and snapped it in two. "I'm going to make love to that delectable pussy with my mouth and my tongue and my fingers but I'm going to do it on *my* time, because when I finally sink balls-deep into you, it's going to be hard, fast and without mercy."

Her thighs trembled. "Fuck, Mateo."

"That'll come later." He pushed aside the torn remains of her thong, exposing her glistening folds to his hungry gaze.

If it had been possible, Olivia would have come just from the look on Mateo's face as he watched her spread open before him. It wasn't reverence. It wasn't lust. It was a mix of both and something she couldn't identify that softened the hard lines in his face even as desire turned his hazel eyes dark green.

Heat swamped her body as potent as the thickest August humidity and sweat beaded against her skin while she waited for him to make his next move. It was nearly more than she could bear.

"Mateo," she moaned, the desperate desire turning her liquid and pliant, making her voice breathy.

Raising his gaze up to her face, he slid a single finger into her opening, circling it so it rubbed against every millimeter of her as if he were exploring uncharted territory. Her thighs quivered, recognizing a familiar master at work. She lifted her hips in an effort to take more of him in, but he rested his forearm across her, right above her pubic bone, forcing her ass back against the island. His weight as he pressed down added to the intensity of the electric sensation sizzling up from her core as he toyed with her.

It may have been years since they'd done this, but he hadn't lost a step. The man loved to torment her as much as he liked to take her higher than she'd ever been with anyone else.

"What do you want?" he asked.

As if he didn't know. As if it wasn't the same thing he wanted.

"I want you inside me." She *needed* to be filled by him, stretched to her limit and taken even further. It's what she'd always needed: Mateo and no one else.

"Like this?" A second finger joined the first, working in tandem, sending delicious shivers through her body. "Oh, look at your pussy clench around me. I think you missed me."

They'd never been exclusive and she'd never been a saint, but no one played her body like Mateo. Hard when she needed it and soft when she wanted it, he'd always fit her as if their bodies knew something their heads didn't. That's what had made his banishment of her from his life after the accident so heartbreaking. They may have pretended it had been about being fuck buddies, but it never had been—that connection had always been there and it hadn't gone anywhere. She'd never stopped loving him and now in Salvation, they'd found their way back to each other again.

"So slick. So soft. Let's see how you taste." He removed his arm from across her hips then pulled her outer lips wide and dipped his tongue into her, lapping at her folds as if they were covered in cream.

The heady sensations were nearly overwhelming as he teased her clit and twisted his fingers, sliding them in and out of her pussy. They zipped up her spine, making her back arch and drawing a hungry moan from her throat.

"Even better than I remembered." He glided his tongue across her clit, hard enough to push her to the edge but soft enough to leave her wavering on it without going over.

Breath coming in short gasps, she grabbed the edges of her skirt that he'd tossed up around her waist and fisted the material, needing something to hold on to because her sanity was slipping away. "It's not nice to tease."

He blew against her swollen clit. "Who said I was nice?"

Before she could form a response, he was back at it—his mouth, tongue and fingers everywhere, at once or at least that's how it felt as an electric current ran through her body, jolting everything from her mind except for the magic Mateo was performing between her legs. The scratch of his unshaved cheeks against her sensitive flesh, pricking her already-taut nerve endings. The wet warmth of his tongue circling her clit until her whole body throbbed. The hard thrust of his fingers as he plunged inside her, rubbing in just the right spot with each forward and reverse.

The pulsing started in her core, slow and steady, building with every breath she inhaled until her entire body thrummed. He took her closer and closer to that edge with each touch, each lick, each unspoken promise of what was to come next until there was no next—there was only now and the pleasure pulsing through her as her orgasm broke and she came apart.

A blissful haze surrounded her, making any movement nearly impossible, but she couldn't let it take over just yet. She needed more. She needed Mateo. Sitting up, she gathered her bearings back here on planet earth.

He stood between her legs, a lusty gleam darkening his eyes, her juices on his lips and a raging hard-on tenting his shorts. But instead of whipping his shorts off, he tugged her upturned skirt back in place and took a step away from her. There was something in his face she didn't recognize, a hesitance she'd never associated with Mateo—definitely not when it came to sex.

It hit her dead between the eyes. She couldn't ask if she was the last woman he'd been with, not without all of his defenses locking into place, but it made sense. They'd met at the hotel a few weeks before the explosion in Afghanistan. After that, his life had been hospitals and a homecoming to a town he'd never wanted to come back to with a face he didn't recognize when he looked in the mirror. She clamped her teeth together hard enough to make her jaw ache so she wouldn't say anything stupid. Mateo didn't admit to or show vulnerability, before or after his injuries. Bringing up what he would see as a weakness would only push him further away, and she was done with that. They had a second chance together, a do-over on life; she just had to get him to see that. He wouldn't listen to her words, but she could make him feel the truth with her body.

She hopped down from the island and reached around to lower the zipper at the back of her skirt. She shimmied her hips and the material slid down her legs and landed in a pool at her feet. Slowly, she slid a bra strap down, then the other, before reaching behind her for the hooks holding it up. A second later her bra joined her skirt on the floor. "Sit down in that chair."

He crossed his arms over that fabulously muscular chest of his, making his biceps bulge. "Since when do you get to give orders?"

Doing her best catwalk strut, her breasts swaying with each stomping step forward, she strutted to him. Stopping just short of his broad chest, she snagged the elastic waistband of his shorts and pulled it as far away from his washboard abs as it would go.

"Ever since I decided that I'm going to be the one to ride first. I want to watch you as I take that big cock of yours inside me and rock back and forth on it until you come so hard your toes will stay curled for a week." She let go of his shorts and they snapped back against his abs with a satisfying crack. "Now take those off."

The chair was hard, cold and uncomfortable as hell, but Mateo didn't give a shit—not when Olivia stood in front of him. She looked even better naked than he remembered. Her curves had softened, become more pronounced since she'd given up modeling, but it wasn't just that. The way she held herself was different. Any element of performance was gone, replaced by a confidence that was sexier than anything he'd ever seen.

"I'll let you have your way this once." He reached down and circled his hard cock, giving it a slow stroke.

Her gaze followed his movements and she licked her lips. "How big of you."

"Big, huh?" His dick thickened under her hot, assessing gaze. "I suppose I am."

While keeping her legs straight, she put her hands on his thighs, bent over, lowered her head and licked the pre-come off his prick. The view straight up her back with her round ass high in the air was phenomenal, but the feel of her tongue as she lapped up the liquid from the head of his prick ripped a moan of appreciation from his throat. Then she took him inside her warm mouth and he couldn't watch her anymore. If he looked as she slid her pink lips up and down his cock, he'd blow before he ever got a chance to slide inside her. He needed to grab a cond–

"Shit!" He yelled out the word in frustration.

Olivia popped her head up, replacing her lips with her fingers as she stroked his dick. "What's wrong?"

"I don't have a condom." His hand didn't require one and that was the only partner he'd had in three years. "I haven't needed one since before..."

His throat closed up. He couldn't say it out loud. It was too fucking pathetic. The woman who'd rocked his world like no others was naked in front of him, wanting nothing more but to fuck him blind, and he couldn't do a damn thing about it. He'd pushed her away at that hotel three years ago like the cocky bastard he'd been, so sure she'd be waiting for him when he came back. Maybe this was his proper penance for his sins, to get so close and not be able to feel her— *really* feel her—again.

She straightened and then stepped over his legs so she straddled him. “I’m on the Pill.”

His heart screeched to a halt in his chest before revving back up like a race car hitting the straightaway. “Are you sure you want to do this?”

Bracing her hands on his shoulders, she lowered herself down onto his straining cock, sheathing him completely in one long, torturously amazing stroke.

“Does that answer your question?” she asked.

Tight. She was so fucking tight around him, the perfect fit. The last blood cells powering his brain fled south where all the fun was going on and he switched into primal mode. He gripped her hips, lifting her and slamming her back down against him, hard and fast. The absolute rightness of it swept through him, Olivia might not be his, no matter how much he wished she was, but she was his for right now and he was going to make sure she knew it.

“Oh my God, Mateo.” She rocked against him on the downward thrust as her nails dug into his shoulders. “Yes. Fuck me. Fuck me hard.”

“You want it hard?” It’s what he promised when everything had started and he wanted—needed—to deliver.

She nodded. “Please.”

Then that’s just what she’d get. He yanked her off his cock and got up from the chair. Olivia stood in front of him, her chest heaving and a confused, lust-dazed look on her face. Evidence of her desire glistened on her inner thighs and her nipples jutted out from her tits. Oh yes, she wanted it just as much as he did.

This wasn't a pity fuck. This was a welcome home. Finally.

He strode behind her and then stepped close enough that his chest pressed against her back and his hard-on nestled between her ass cheeks. Dipping his head lower, he brought his lips to the outer shell of her ear. "Face the chair and kneel on it."

She shivered against him before doing what he asked.

Tracing a finger down the length of her spine, he wondered at the fact that, of all the people in the world who should run away from him, it was Olivia who stayed with him even when he tried to scare her away. It had always been like that, with her and only her. The realization warmed a spot inside him that had been dark and frozen for years. "Hold on to the chair, honey."

She curled her fingers around the back of the chair, spread her knees apart as far as possible and arched her back so her ass was offered up like the gift it was.

The sight made it impossible to move and barely allowed breath to enter his constricted lungs. "Damn, you are so beautiful."

She peeked over her shoulder and shot him a saucy smirk. "Stop staring and give me your cock."

"This cock?" He gripped his prick and smacked her ass with it.

"Yes." Her heady sigh just egged him on.

"You want it?" *Smack. Smack. Smack.*

"Yes," she cried, hungry and demanding.

The time for teasing had passed. His beauty needed relief, and she wasn't the only one. He eased into her, taking his time until he was balls-deep.

Relishing the feel of her tight hold on his dick, he paused for a breath but the buzzing at the base of his spine grew with each inhale as he held the position, until he couldn't take it anymore. He had to move, had to feel her come all over him.

Back and forth, he rocked his hips, slamming into her as she pushed back against him, meeting him thrust for thrust. Hard and fast, bordering on desperate, their bodies crashed together until she tossed her head back and came, screaming his name.

That's all it took. His balls tightened and he thrust forward, his orgasm spilling into her harder than he'd ever come before.

Mateo wrapped his arms around her waist and lifted her as he pivoted so he sat on the chair with her nestled on his lap. She settled her cheek into the pocket of his shoulder.

"You'd better not move for a good long while," she mumbled as her eyes fluttered shut.

He brushed a kiss against her hair and tightened his hold on her, making sure she was secure on his lap. "Don't worry, you belong right here, love."

His lungs seized. *Love.* It had just slipped out. But she hadn't noticed. Her breathing never changed and she didn't open her eyes as he held her close and tried to process the truth his body had recognized long before his head.

Not that there was anything to be done about it. Olivia was meant for a better man than the beast he'd become.

Chapter Ten

Steam thickened the air in the bathroom as Olivia toweled herself dry after the shower. Bending at the waist, she stretched down, touching her toes to help relieve the lingering aches from falling asleep in such an awkward position last night. How Mateo made it as long as he did, holding her on his lap as he sat in that hard kitchen chair, she had no idea. She'd woken up hours later as he carried her up the stairs to his room, the dog trailing behind.

Staying over hadn't been her plan when she'd arrived last night armed with two slices of pecan pie—shit, fucking Mateo in his kitchen hadn't been her plan—and yet she'd woken up in his arms. It was as if she couldn't resist, as if being with him was inevitable. The thought should scare the ever-loving shit out of her. It didn't.

Still basking in the glow of last night's double-orgasm high, she felt as if anything was possible. Today she was going to persuade the Salvation holdouts to support the veterans' center fundraiser. It was a win for the vets, for the town, and for the little Sweet on his or her way. Everything was going to work out.

A knock sounded just as she was wrapping a large, fluffy towel around her body.

"I have a T-shirt for you, if you want to borrow it," Mateo said through the closed door.

Just the sound of his voice sent a delicious shiver through her and tightened her nipples into hard points. "You mean you don't want to watch me run naked across that back field to the cabin so I can get dressed?"

"I do now. I'm going to go burn all the clothing in the house except for a couple of old ties so I can secure you to the bed."

"You're so funny." She whipped open the door. "Give up the shirt."

The dog trotted in, sniffing the strawberry scent lingering in the air from her body wash and licking the last drops of water from her toes. Olivia barely noticed the tickle because just looking at Mateo, again dressed only in basketball shorts, put her on sensory overload. The man should never be allowed to wear a shirt. Or shorts. Or really anything at all.

He gave her a slow up-and-down perusal while fisting the gray T-shirt. "Breakfast is ready."

"You made me breakfast?" That had never happened before. Hotel room service? Yes. Restaurant? Occasionally. Anything not delivered by someone wearing a name tag? Never.

The tops of his ears turned pink. "Don't get too excited, it's toaster waffles and juice."

"Sounds perfect."

He turned to go, obviously in retreat mode.

"Hey, Mateo," she called out.

He spun around. "Yeah?"

She held out her hand. "The shirt?"

He looked down as if he'd forgotten what he'd been holding. A wicked smile curled his lips as he looked back up at her, his gaze stopping on the spot right between her breasts where she'd secured her towel as if he could flick it open with just a glance. Instead, he gave her a slow wink and handed over the shirt. "See you downstairs."

Awareness singed her skin and her breath caught in her chest. Before, they'd always been rushing, her from catwalk to catwalk and him from battlefield to battlefield, stopping only long enough to meet, fuck and begin the countdown until the next time. Maybe this time they'd both stay put long enough to actually see if what was between them could work for more than a stolen weekend at a hotel.

Mateo thought giving her the shirt would help end his perma-boner. Then Olivia sauntered through the kitchen in the T-shirt that barely covered her pert ass and he realized the immense error of his ways. All the thin cotton did was make him remember every single detail of what was underneath. She was killing him with her hotness. Slowly. Thoroughly. Ruthlessly.

"Wow," she chuckled. "That's a lot of waffles."

He looked down at the stack of eight on his plate. "I'm hungry."

She stopped behind him, wrapped her arms around his waist and pressed her cheek to his bare back. "You did have a helluva workout last night."

Before he could make a snappy rejoined, that weirdo cat of hers jumped up on the island and started stalking Mateo's breakfast. He slid a protective arm around his plate, marking his territory.

It was just enough movement to make the dog lift his sleepy head, give the air a quick sniff, realize company had arrived and go berserk.

Chaos erupted. Barks and hisses as the cat peered over the edge of the island and glared at the dog. Wagging tails and sharp claws as the dog jumped and spun in place with the cat taking swipes whenever it could. Total fucking insanity ensued as the fur flew when the cat made contact.

He and Olivia jumped apart. He grabbed the dog's collar while she scooped up the cat. For half a breath, sanity returned. Then the three-legged cat sprung from Olivia's grasp and skedaddled right out the open back door. The dog broke Mateo's hold and sped out after the feline.

All Mateo could do was wonder what in the hell had just happened. "Want me to go after them?"

Olivia peeked out of the window and shook her head. "It's okay. Handsome's perched on top of the shed."

He laughed. He couldn't help it. The unfamiliar sound just bubbled up inside of him and erupted out. "You named that ugly thing Handsome?"

"At least he has a name." She grabbed a mug from the counter and poured herself some coffee. You need to give one to the dog."

"He's not mine." He'd said it a thousand times, but each denial was becoming weaker.

"Don't tell him that, he'd be heartbroken." She sat down on one of the stools surrounding the island and sipped her steaming coffee as she looked out the window at her cat ignoring the dog, who was still losing his damn mind. The sun caught in her hair, turning the honey strands golden.

The whole scene was foreign to him. In the days before his last fateful tour, he'd never had women stay the night. He'd always gone to their place or a hotel. It just kept things neater; the less involvement, the cleaner it would be when he walked away—and he'd always walked away.

Even from Olivia, the single person he'd spent years running toward, if only for a weekend at a time.

By the time he'd realized what an idiot he'd been for turning down her offer of making their arrangement more like a relationship, he was in a strange country with the explosion ringing in his ears and his friends' blood dripping down his face.

Yet here he was, sitting in his kitchen with Olivia, and instead of rushing her out the door, the urge to linger had him glued to his stool. Maybe her coming back to Salvation wasn't his penance. Maybe it was a second chance...if he had the balls to go after it.

"Breakfast." He pushed a plate of waffles her way as he tried to figure out what to say. Small talk wasn't in his wheelhouse. It wasn't even in the same country. So he blurted out the first thing that came into his mind. "Explain to me why this fundraiser is such a big deal for you. It looks like it's been nothing but headaches so far. Why not just say fuck it?"

She used her fork to slide her cut-up waffles around her plate, refusing to look up at him. "I can't."

No doubt Olivia had secondary motives for the fundraiser, but he couldn't make Hawson's theory about it all being a plot to get her back into the spotlight jive with the woman nervously chewing a hole in her bottom lip. "Why not?"

"Between us?"

He nodded, not liking the way her body was curling inward as if she could hide inside herself. His dormant protector instinct woke and stomped its way up from the deep dark hole where he'd buried it.

Olivia set her fork down on her plate, folded her hands in her lap and raised her face so their gazes locked. "Miranda's pregnant."

How this hadn't made the gossip rounds at The Kitchen Sink yet, he had no idea. That was some CIA-level secret-keeping there. "And you think rebuilding the veterans' center will make the town think better of your family before the new member comes along."

"Exactly." Her face lit up and the hope he saw in her blue eyes punched him right in the kidney.

Her plan made sense in a convoluted Sweet sort of way, but the town mayor had super-villain level determination when it came to keeping Salvation as his personal Sweet-hating fiefdom. "You're in trouble."

"Really?" She snorted. "I hadn't noticed."

"You've got to figure out a way to outflank Hawson." And the mayor was loaded for bear. It wasn't going to be easy.

"If only I could just—"

She suddenly jumped off her stool and did an excited shimmy dance that lifted the T-shirt up to her hips, showing off everything that was bare beneath. "That's it!"

"What's it?" He shifted. Now was not the time for his dick to go back to aching hardness.

"I just need to get some face time with people." She paced from one end of the kitchen to the other, gesturing wildly with her hands as she talked out her plan of attack. "If I can convince them that this is a win-win for everyone, then the veterans will get a new center and the town won't have the ruined building as an eyesore."

"And your niece or nephew may have a better reception from Salvation than you or your sisters did."

She stopped in her tracks and the hopeful light that had lit her up from the inside flickered. "The problem is, how do I get folks to sit down with me? No one showed up for the volunteer training."

Shock and awe wasn't what she needed. It was hearts and minds time. "You need to go one-on-one and forge relationships in hostile territory. You can do it, but having an envoy might help."

"I could ask Logan. His family has been here forever."

"Sounds like there's a but coming..."

"I really wanted to prove to my sisters that I wasn't the total flake I'd been in the past—you know, the one who brought a documentary film crew home for Christmas and ended up embarrassing the whole town. This fundraiser is also a way to show that I have the chops to bring something useful to the brewery. I'm good at marketing. I can help, and now that the boxes aren't packed floor to ceiling in my office, this is my chance."

"I can take you around to a couple of places." The words were out of his mouth before he thought twice.

"Last night wasn't about buttering you up. The pecan pie was, but afterwards, that was just us."

Judging by the way she'd come apart in his arms last night, he didn't doubt her for a second. "I'll remember that next time you bring me pie."

Cupping his face in her hands, she kissed him long and slow before pulling away. "Thank you."

"I'm just your driver." He shrugged. "Don't depend on me for anything else."

Three days later, Olivia shielded her eyes from the setting sun as she and Mateo walked down Phillip Deckerson's front porch steps and mentally added one more person to her list of fundraiser supporters, which brought the number up to twenty five. All in all, a pretty damn successful day.

She managed to close the SUV's passenger door before the giggles spilled out from between her lips. "Oh my God, did you see the look on his face when I said Tyrell Hawson's name? I thought fire was going to come shooting out of his nose."

Mateo fastened his seat belt. "Nothing like a bogus eminent domain claim by the city to get an old man's back up."

"Thank you for this." She fiddled with the seat belt, a familiar fluttering in her stomach—one that always seemed to make its presence known whenever she was around him.

She'd done all the talking but it was Mateo who'd gotten her in the door. When they weren't arguing or tearing each other's clothes off, they made a pretty damn good team. Was that how love worked? Maybe it did for them.

"Don't worry, I'll figure out a way to make you pay me back." His stomach growled as he turned onto Main Street. "But first, dinner and then some pie."

"I don't know what Ruby Sue puts in it, but it's addictive." She giggled. "I think you need to investigate."

"If by 'investigate', you mean eat it, then I'm all for it."

Mateo pulled into The Kitchen Sink's parking lot and stopped next to a cherry-red sports car near the front door that made her eye twitch.

It couldn't be.

He'd already fucked-up her life, what was left for her ex to ruin?

Her hand shook as she grasped the handle and pushed the door open. She held her breath as she stepped out onto the asphalt lot and looked around for signs of Larry.

"You okay?" Mateo asked after coming to stand by her on the sidewalk leading to the diner.

Giving the outside of the diner one last look, she turned her gaze to Mateo. "I'm sure it's noth—"

The Kitchen Sink's door opened and her ex-boyfriend stepped out, wearing a bespoke suit and a slimy grin. Whatever the hell she'd seen in him, she had no idea. The man was a generic pretty boy with a gambling problem and an ugly heart. Compared to Mateo, he was nothing but smoke and mirrors.

Larry paused outside the door and withdrew a cigarette from a half-empty pack. "Hey there, good looking."

It took a second for her brain to process that the man who'd posted pictures of her playing with her breasts on a revenge-porn site was standing within bitch-slapping distance. However, once it did, a white-hot anger blasted through her body, hot enough to turn her lungs to toast. Her hands curled into fists and she took a step forward before her mind caught up with her body. Beating the shit out of the scumbag would feel good, but it wouldn't help her. The last thing she needed after working Salvation like a politician on election day was to remind everyone in town how crazy the Sweet girls could be. As good as it would feel to slap the smug look off Larry's smug face, it wasn't worth what it would cost her future niece or nephew.

"What in the hell are you doing here?" she snarled.

Seemingly unaffected by her reaction, Larry lit his cigarette and took a slow drag before bothering to answer. "Is that any way to greet your boyfriend?"

"*Ex*-boyfriend, Larry." Fury ate at her until even her hair vibrated with barely leashed rage. "That's what happens when you post naked pictures of me to the web, get me fired from my job, empty out our joint account and sell everything else to pay off your gambling debts."

"You shouldn't hold grudges; especially not against someone giving you a chance to get back something you want."

"You're kidding, right?" Her nails bit into her palms, the pain helping to keep her temper on lockdown. "It's a little too late for that, don't you think? The damn pictures are already on the internet."

Larry tilted his chin toward the sky and blew a series of smoke rings. "This time it's a video, not pictures of your tit-jiggling show."

"Watch it." Mateo took a threatening step forward, chest puffed out and a look on his face that would send smarter men than her ex scurrying for cover.

Instead, the idiot tossed his cigarette down and stubbed it out. "Cool it there, Two-Face. My business is with the chick, not you."

She slid between the two posturing men, ready to claw Larry's face to pieces herself. "Larry, I'm going to string you up by your balls if you don't get the hell out of Salvation."

"I will as soon as you pay me for the video."

The man was unbalanced; he had to be. " *You're* the one who emptied our accounts. I don't have anything left."

"You better find some or the world is going to be fapping to this." He held out his phone, keeping it angled so that *she* could see the video playing, but not Mateo.

She glanced down. A black-and-white video of an elevator interior played. A man and a woman were in one corner. At first it didn't register—and then the memory came rushing back.

Her and Mateo's last night before his deployment. The striptease in the elevator.

Fear and panic squeezed her chest hard enough that she was surprised her ribs didn't crack under the pressure. If this got out, everything would be ruined. Mateo would never forgive her for putting him under such an unsavory spotlight. The town would turn its back on the fundraiser and the Sweet family. Her future niece or nephew would grow up under the same harsh community glare that she and her sisters had.

"How?" It took a supreme effort just to get the single word out.

Larry smirked. "A source at the hotel contacted me after he saw the photos of you that I had posted.

I paid a pretty penny for this. You're going to repay me for that, plus interest, and then you'll get the file."

Chapter Eleven

Pounding this douchebag into an over-cologned pulp sounded good to Mateo. Too good—especially for a police chief. So instead, he stepped closer to Olivia and placed a comforting hand on the small of her back while giving her ex the death stare.

The guy did a double take and took a step back, which was the first smart thing the prick had done since he'd had the balls to talk to Olivia.

"Oh my God, it's *you,*" Larry gasped. "The dude in the video. It took me a second but it's definitely you. Damn man, what happened?"

The world jarred to a stop. "What video?"

"The before and after of this could jack up the interest," Larry said as he eyeballed Mateo's scars, as if he could catalog each crooked line. "Some people really go for that kind of thing."

Olivia stepped out of his embrace. "Larry, stop. Please." Her voice trembled. She pivoted in his arms, unshed tears pooling in her blue eyes. "I'm sorry, Mateo. I had nothing to do with this. Really."

Nothing made sense beyond the fact that this dirtbag had a video that could turn Olivia from a fighter to a woman on the verge of tears. "What video?"

"This one." Larry flipped his cell phone around.

It was a little grainy and in black and white, but there was no mistaking Olivia in a trench coat dress that he'd remember on his death bed—leather, red and easily unwrapped. She'd strutted into that bar and the rest of the world had ceased to exit, including the security cameras in the elevator.

Up until the end, it had been the greatest night he'd ever had until last night—and now some douchebag who thought blackmail was an enviable skill was treating that moment like it was a dirty bargaining chip.

On the phone, Mateo turned, revealing the unmarred left side of his face, the way it would never be again. It was the face of a cocky asshole who thought the world would always fall at his feet; the overconfident jerk who never thought that one bad judgement call would result in his team turning into a bloody mist in front of his eyes; and the idiot who didn't realize how much Olivia meant to him until he'd pushed her away.

Olivia's image on the phone caught his eye. How could he see the love so clearly on her face now when in person he'd missed it completely?

Because now his outside matched his inside: ugly and unworthy of Olivia. She deserved better than the cocksure pretty boy he'd been and she sure as hell deserved more than the scarred wreck of a man he'd become. The best thing he could do for her to make up for it all was to get out of her life.

"Larry, you're a real piece of shit." Olivia grabbed at the phone, but her ex pulled it away before she could yank it out of his hand.

"I can live with that as long as you give me my money," he replied.

"You *took* all of my money, you moron." Olivia trembled with anger.

" *Our* money, and that's too bad." Larry's eyes narrowed into strips of evil intent. "I already have buyers on the line."

That was it.

Mateo swiped Larry's phone out of his hand and threw it to the ground. It exploded, sending pieces of plastic flying into the air.

Larry responded with a haymaker that barely grazed Mateo's chin.

Mateo grabbed the other man by his collar and jerked him close. "That video never sees the light of day. If it does, you'll just wish you were dead because it would be a helluva lot better than the pain I would rain down on you. Do you copy?"

"Ease up, man; it's not a big deal." Larry squirmed ineffectively. "Everyone will congratulate you for banging her and think *she's* a slut for getting naked in the elevator."

Olivia gasped and clasped her hand to her mouth.

A fierce rage erupted from a dark place in Mateo's soul, pouring through him like the hottest lava, scorching his control until all that was left was its charred remains. He hauled Larry up until his tiptoes barely touched the sidewalk. "No one talks about her like that. No. One."

He slammed the dirtbag against The Kitchen Sink's brick wall hard enough that the impact vibrated up his forearms. Then he did it again. And again. He curled his hands into fists and landed a right hook against the other man's check. He deflected a weak punch and then followed with a pair of jabs that landed square in the man's soft belly. By the time he stepped back, Larry was breathing hard, a shiner darkened one eye and blood dripped from the corner of his mouth.

The urge to keep going rushed through Mateo, pounding against his brain and refusing to be ignored. But he had to. He was the police chief. What he'd done—though deserved—was bad enough. There would be consequences, for him *and* for Olivia.

"Get out of here," Mateo said, his fists heavy as iron by his side. "And don't come back."

"I'm going to sell this video for cheap now." He spit a bloody glob of phlegm on the sidewalk, nearly hitting Olivia's shoe. "See you at the movies, skank."

Red ate away the edges of his vision. "You really are a stupid motherfucker."

Mateo's fist crashed against Larry's nose. Bone crunched under the impact. The other man stumbled back, but Mateo wasn't letting him get far. He'd had his chance to escape and had blown it. His fist landed an uppercut to the guy's cheekbone. His head snapped back.

"Stop, Mateo!" Olivia grabbed his arm. "You have to stop."

He swung his arm in a wide arc to shake off her hold. He couldn't stop, it was too late now. Once again, he'd fucked-up someone else's life because of his poor choices. He'd gotten the penthouse suite. He'd talked her into undressing in the elevator. He'd said no when she'd asked for more. The anger and frustration filled him to the bursting point. It needed an outlet and Larry made the perfect target.

Again and again, his fists found their home as the other man struggled to stay up. Then, as Larry wavered on his feet, Mateo landed a solid punch to the other man's jaw, knocking him flat on his ass. Mateo stood over him, adrenaline rushing through his veins and roaring in his ears. But he wasn't staring down at Olivia's scumbag ex-boyfriend.

"Chief!" The voice sounded so far away.

All he could see was the bloody mess of Ferrante and Hamilton and Washington and Perth after the IED explosion. Stopping to help the kid, who couldn't have been more than four, had seemed like the right thing to do. He was so young, sitting in the middle of the road and crying. Matteo had gotten out of the vehicle and approached with caution. He'd held out his hand and helped the kid up. That's what had trigged the bomb—the kid standing.

"Chief!" The voice was louder this time.

He looked over. Simons. What was his grandmotherly dispatcher doing in Afghanistan?

"Chief, I need you to stand down."

Blinking, he brought the world around him—the real world—back into focus. Bloody and bruised, Larry cupped his jaw as he got back to his feet. A crowd had spilled out of The Kitchen Sink, surrounding them. An ambulance siren grew steadily louder as it approached.

Belly turning into poisoned lead, he pivoted to face Olivia—and nearly threw up. A red mark slashed its way across her cheek. That split second when she'd tried to stop him and he'd shaken her off flashed in his mind. *He* must have done that to her.

"Olivia. I never meant—" He took a step forward, but Simons curled her fingers around his arm, holding him back.

"I need you to come with me, Chief," Simons said, her voice a little too calm and too kind. "Just get in the cruiser here and we'll get all this straightened out back at the station."

He couldn't look away from Olivia and the fear in her blue eyes. He'd put it there. Defending her honor had seemed like the right thing to do, but all he'd done was make things worse. He hadn't realized until right now just how right he'd been that night in the hotel, when he'd told her he wasn't someone who could be depended on. And a woman like Olivia deserved that; she deserved more than him, even if he *was* the sad sap in love with her.

That's what it was, what it always had been, from that first hotel getaway—love. Now it was too late. He had to sever ties, permanently. It was the best thing he could do for her.

Cutting his gaze away from her, he turned and walked to the cruiser. He reached for the door handle and noticed that his knuckles were swollen and bloody. They should hurt like a bitch but he didn't feel a damn thing. He hoped he never would again.

Fear for Mateo ate away at Olivia as she rubbed her cheek, bruised from stumbling into the brick wall, and followed him toward the police car. A small hand wrapped around her wrist, stopping her.

"Nothing you can do for him right now," Ruby Sue said as she tugged her back toward The Kitchen Sink's front door. "Best thing to do is to get your ducks in a row for bail."

Still trying to process what had just happened, her brain hiccupped. "Bail?"

Ruby Sue shook her head. "Come on, girl, it hasn't been that long since you had to get your parents out of the county jail."

"More than ten years." Her dad had protested the closure of the drama club, her most loved extracurricular activity, by sitting down buck naked on the fifty-yard line during the high school homecoming game.

Ruby Sue shrugged. "When you're my age, ten years is an eye blink. Come on inside, we'll get you some pie and figure out what to do next."

They weaved their way through the gossiping crowd surrounding Larry as the paramedic evaluated his obviously broken nose. Everyone there was determined to get a good look at the damage Mateo had inflicted, no doubt so they could exaggerate it sufficiently at the Boot Scoot Boogie honky tonk later that night.

The cold march of ants up her spine told her the exact moment Larry spotted her in the crowd. She knew she shouldn't look. She should just keep moving.

"Unless you come up with the cash," he hollered, "I'm going to sell that video to the lowest bidder!"

Something inside her snapped and she jerked to a stop. After everything, he still thought he could cow her into doing what he wanted. The man was a moron, and so was she for ever thinking she saw something in him. The crowd buzzed around her. She and her sisters may be the only Sweets left in Salvation, but the town still knew what Larry had no clue about. You could push a Sweet only so far before they let their freak flag fly and invited the world to come sit down and see all their ugly up close.

The initial blast of anger gave way to a crystal clear understanding of what had to happen next. He thought he had a bargaining chip? He had nothing, and she was going to show him just how little of nothing he had.

"You lost whatever hold you had over me with this video when I came back home. In Salvation, I'm just one more in a long line of crazy Sweets. We're *expected* to do things that cross the lines like get naked in an elevator. Hell, my grandmother allegedly burned down the DMV; we, of course, maintain it was an electrical fire. Do you really think that video would harm my reputation in *this* town?" She laughed. Hard. For once, being an unhinged Sweet was going to work in her favor. "You want to sell that video? Go for it."

"I will." He tried to smirk but the way his lips were swelling up made it impossible.

Now to turn the screws. "Just remember that everyone here heard you threaten me unless I gave you cash. That's blackmail."

"Semantics." He shrugged, but his gaze darted around the crowd as if confirming they'd heard. "I was giving you first right of refusal."

"The cops won't see it that way. Not to mention that video wasn't a gift to you, so you can't sell it like you did the photos. You stole it from a hotel's security system. I may not be able to hire every attorney on the West Coast to go after you for that theft, but I bet a massive high-end hotel chain like that one can." She paused to let her words sink into his thick skull. "After all, they don't want their guests to think they sell security footage to the highest bidder."

"They wouldn't come after me." His voice was firm but there was no missing the sweat making his forehead wet.

"And that's just civil penalties." Time to bring it home and scare the ever-loving shit out of Larry so well that he'd never bother her again. "The theft would still catch the prosecuting attorney's eye—especially a high-profile, sexy case like this would be. I still know a lot of media folks and I won't be the least bit shy in asking them for coverage. Everyone in the western hemisphere would know what a scumbag you are and that the video is stolen goods. You'd never be able to sell it. Even the shittiest of porn sites would know not to touch you with a twenty-foot pole dipped in hydrogen peroxide. Face it, that video is worthless."

Heart hammering in her chest, Olivia savored the rush that went with taking an asshole down a couple pegs or twenty. Then she turned on her heel and left, leaving Larry and more than a couple of gawkers with their mouths hanging open, and stormed into The Kitchen Sink. Only a few people remained inside, including her least-favorite mayor, Tyrell Hawson. Just the sight of him leeched some of the fuck-yeah adrenaline from her. The man sucked the joy out of everything.

Unlike the others, who were glued to the diner's front windows, he sat with his back to the hubbub outside and sipped coffee from a bright-red mug. "Looks like your chickens have come home to roost and have shit all over our police chief. He had a promising career going until you came back to town."

Mateo. Her gut twisted. She hadn't thought of his job. An arrest was a day that ended in Y for previous generations of Sweets, but not so for the Salvation Police Chief.

She lowered her voice, hoping against logic that the few people in the diner weren't doing everything they could to overhear. "Larry took the first swing."

"Looked to me like your protector returned a lot more than one swing's worth." He glanced up from his half-empty coffee mug. "Oh no, our police chief is done carrying a badge, unless someone who has a lot of influence were to go to bat for him."

She snorted. "Someone like you."

"Now that you mention it, that does sound like me." His lips curled in a cruel mockery of a smile.

The air wheezed out of her lungs and she sank down onto the chair next to his. How did she get here? Bargaining with the man who loved to bedevil the Sweets at every turn. "What do you want?"

"Cancel the fundraiser for the veterans' center."

"But that's something *good* that will benefit the whole town. Why does your hatred for my family outweigh the good we can do?"

He sat his mug down on the counter and swiveled his chair so he faced her. Loathing rolled off him in waves as a crimson flush crept up his neck.

"Because you're bad for Salvation," he snarled. "Your family likes to think of themselves as eccentrics with hearts of gold who are involved in criminal hijinks, but to me, your people are the broken windows in a neighborhood. You're the first sign of things going downhill. Fool that he is, out there, Mateo was trying to protect your reputation—as if that was possible. Well, I'm trying to protect this town so that it grows and prospers. If your family name is connected to anything like the veterans' center, it will only tarnish Salvation."

By the time he was done, Tyrell's round cheeks were bright red with bitter frustration. It wasn't just a power grab, an ego trip, or revenge for the Christmas special documentary crew that had caught him dancing with his horse. He really believed what he was saying. There'd be no convincing him otherwise. He'd keep fighting her every step of the way—and he wasn't above fighting dirty and taking down anyone who got in his way.

"Cancel the fundraiser. That's it?" She pictured Miranda's rounding belly and her throat tightened. Then she imagined Mateo handing in his badge and going to jail because of her.

He nodded. "One word from me and the judge sets a low bail and dismisses the charges. Then everything goes back to normal." He narrowed his eyes. "Do we have a deal?"

She nodded, unable to get words past the lump in her throat.

"Good. I'll go speak to the judge." He stood and took a few steps toward the door then stopped and pivoted back to look at her. "Don't think about double-crossing me. I'm not the kind of enemy you want to have."

Sunset's last orange hues were barely visible in the western sky when the dog picked his head up off Olivia's lap and jumped down from where they'd been snuggling in the porch swing. Handsome, perched on the porch railing, executed a deep feline stretch and stared out into the darkened driveway. Headlights pierced the night as Mateo's truck rumbled up the gravel road.

Her hands shook as she brushed them across her favorite yellow skirt and stood. Waiting on the porch after she'd called Luciana to let her know Mateo had been taken into custody had been the longest hours of her life. Against her better judgement, she'd pinned all her hopes on the mayor delivering on his end of the bargain, and he had. Relief swept through her as she released the breath she'd been holding since he'd started up the drive.

Mateo got out of the Salvation Police Department SUV, stopping at the back bumper and stared at her. Awareness sparked between them, making the rest of the world disappear. This was where she belonged—with the man she loved.

Energy buzzed through her, lightening her steps as she hurried to the railing, ready to call out to him, but something in the ramrod-straight line of his back and the grim twist to his lips stopped her. Dread spread like icy crystals throughout her body.

Not heeding or noticing the undercurrent, the dog went nuts, yapping and hopping along beside Mateo as he made his way stiffly to the front porch.

He glanced up at her cheek and winced. "Are you okay?" He reached out but stopped before his fingers grazed her bruised cheek. "I never meant to hurt you."

"You didn't." She pressed her hand to the bruise; the swelling was already going down. "When you swung your arm free, I stumbled and whacked my cheek against the diner's brick wall." But a scraped cheek wasn't what made her insides twist. "Did they file charges?"

He jammed his fingers through his hair, as if he could shove everything that had happened out of his head. "The whole thing was captured on The Kitchen

Sink's security cameras. You can see him take the first swing and then hear him taunting. The sheriff's office took the case to avoid conflict of interest with my department. They aren't filing charges."

Relief made her shoulders sag. "So what happens now?"

He didn't answer at first. Instead, he climbed up the porch steps and went to the door. After unlocking it, he pushed it open and then turned to face her. "You need to find a new place to live...as far away from me as possible."

Her breath caught and she clasped her hand to the base of her throat. "Mateo, don't—"

"I'm no good for you." He turned away from her, showing her only the scarred left side of his face as he stared straight ahead into his dark house. "I knew it in that hotel room, when I was still whole, but when you came home I let myself forget. I played pretend. Seeing that video brought everything back. I'm not a man anyone should be with, let alone you."

Pulse pounding in her ears, she rushed across the porch, grabbed his arm and forced him to turn and look at her. "Let alone me? What the hell does that mean?"

"It means that I'm a fucking walking disaster!" he roared. "Just look at my face and you can see that. What's even scarier is the fact that I'm the lucky one. The other poor bastards with me ended up dead. And today, I try to help you and I end up making things worse because now your shit of an ex-boyfriend won't just want money, he's gonna want revenge. Just get the fuck out of my life. You don't belong here—you never did and you never will."

He slid his arm free and went into the house, closing the door in her face.

Olivia just stood there, trying to make sense of the world and of the man who she'd loved for most of her life. A numbness drifted over her, the kind she hoped would never go away because that's when the bone-deep pain would hit, hard enough to drop her to her knees.

She couldn't be standing on Mateo's front porch or be in the cabin or even Salvation when it hit.

Scooping up Handsome, she walked to her car. The keys and her purse were still in it. Without thinking about where or how or what next, she got into her Fiat, drove down the driveway and turned left onto the highway. She didn't even look back when she hit the Salvation County line.

Chapter Twelve

The pounding on Mateo's door wouldn't stop. It broke through the hangover headache beating his brain to a pulp and continued relentlessly. He sat up on the couch, still dressed in yesterday's clothes that now stunk of bourbon and shit-ass decisions about his life. The dog had his nose pressed to the bottom of the front door, sniffing, as if whatever was on the other side was better than a T-bone steak.

Olivia.

His pulse ratcheted up and he jumped from the couch. That was how the mutt reacted to her every time—something they both had in common. She'd come back, and he wasn't sure he'd be able to push her away another time. He'd fail her again.

"Mateo Garcia, we know you're in there," Miranda hollered through the door. "Open up right now!"

Relief and disappointment double-punched him in the gut. Not Olivia, her sister. He nudged the dog over with his foot and opened the door.

Both of Olivia's sisters stood on his front porch looking as if they were ready to storm the castle, all they were missing were pitchforks and torches. The dog obviously didn't get the same we're-here-to-slay-you vibe, since it had gone all waggle-butt as it weaved a figure eight around and between the sisters' feet fast enough that he was nearly a blur. Neither Miranda nor Natalie seemed to notice.

"Where is she?" Miranda asked, worry making her voice hard.

"She's not answering her phone," Natalie said.

His stomach dropped to his knees and his chest tightened. "How long?"

"How long what?" Miranda snapped.

"How long since anyone has heard from her?" She was alright. She *had* to be alright.

"Two days." Natalie twisted her fingers around the gold chain circling her neck. "Not since you were arrested."

"She was here when I got home. We had...words. She drove off." Then he'd called in sick and opened the bottle he'd crawled out of this morning. "I'll alert the sheriff's department and the highway patrol to be on the lookout for her car, just in case there was a wreck."

Just the image of her trapped in that ridiculous yellow Fiat at the bottom of a ditch was enough to liquefy his insides.

"You don't think Larry..." Miranda's voice trailed off.

"He left town after the paramedics cleared him." That's why it had taken him so long to get home that night. He'd insisted on following the asshole's car until he crossed the county line. "The deputies, highway patrol and my officers had a BOLO on his car just in case he decided to make a reappearance. He hasn't." He started to close the door. He had to get them out of here, then he'd spend the day combing the back roads looking for any sign of Olivia. "I'll let you know if I hear anything."

"So that brings us back to you." Natalie slapped her hand against the door, stopping him from closing it, and narrowed her gaze. "What did you say to make her leave?"

"The right thing." He shut the door.

It *had* been the right thing. If it hadn't, it wouldn't hurt so much.

The chipper sound of the bells tinkling as he pushed open The Kitchen Sink's door the next day stepped on Mateo's very last nerve. The sun shining so brightly when he'd woken up this morning had stomped on the first. The dog's cheerful, greeting followed by his fruitless search for Olivia in the house for the second day in a row and corresponding whimpers, had obliterated several more. The sight of her strawberry body wash in the shower next to his bottle of plain old no-smell shampoo had snapped more than a handful of nerves right in half.

He'd grabbed the bottle, her shampoo, her conditioner, her pink razor and some fluffy spongy thing hanging from a rope and dumped them all in the trash. It hadn't done a damn thing to make him feel better. He still felt as if a tank had driven over his balls, backed up, and repeated the process until he had pancakes hanging between his legs.

"Well, look who decided to drag his sorry carcass in for lunch," Ruby Sue said from her stool behind the cash register.

He just barely swallowed a snarly comeback. Biting her head off wouldn't fix the FUBAR he'd made of his life by falling in love with Olivia, just like spending twelve hours driving every back-road, highway and country lane in a one-hour radius of Salvation yesterday hadn't turned up even a flash of Olivia's yellow Fiat. "I'll just grab a table in back. I'm meeting Luciana."

She grabbed two menus and led him through the crowded tables toward the booth in the back corner. "So you know half the town figures you have her tied up in some sort of sex dungeon. Personally, I think Olivia skedaddled after you flashed her your ugly."

"Like anyone could miss it," he said, not even trying to keep the bitterness out of his voice as his slid into the booth.

Ruby Sue smacked him on the head with the laminated menu before slapping it down on the table. "I'm talking about the ugly on the inside."

"Look, Ruby Sue." He picked up his menu as if he didn't know every item listed on it and peered over the top at the woman determined to give him a what-for. "I love you, but I'm just not in the mood right now."

"What, to hear that you're acting like a moron? Oh I'm sorry, I didn't mean to hurt your big grumpy-man feelings, but you need to suck it up." She slid into the booth opposite him, her narrow-eyed gaze pinning him in place and burning a hole right through the menu he was pretending to read. "I've been watching you with Olivia. I know what's going on here. Life hurts and love breaks your heart nine times out of ten but when it's that one, then it's a whole other ballgame."

"None of that matters to someone like me." It couldn't. He wouldn't let it.

"What kind of someone is that?"

"One who manages to hurt everyone around him." There. That was the ugly truth of it. He couldn't be depended on because he always failed them in the end.

Ruby Sue reached an arthritic hand across the table and yanked the menu out of his grasp, forcing him to look at her. "Well my goodness, let me go get the bandages with all the cartoon characters on them so I'm prepared for the worst."

All he'd wanted since he got out of the VA hospital was to be left alone, and he'd mostly accomplished that goal until Olivia rolled into town. Now he was trapped in a booth with the Sweet triplets' self-appointed fairy godmother reading him a homespun riot act. There'd be no stopping her until she'd said her piece, so he settled back against the booth. "Just spit out whatever it is you think you need to tell me and then leave me alone."

"Like I need an invitation to tell you what I think." Ruby Sue waved off the approaching waitress. She fiddled with the gold band she always wore around her thumb. A bittersweet look came over her face, as if the ring were both a good luck charm and a curse. "A long time ago, I was engaged to Julian Sweet's eldest brother, Josiah. Oh Lord, that man." She looked up and smiled. It wasn't her usual snarky grin, but a soft smile that gave a glimpse of the woman she'd been decades before. "Tall, dark and handsome didn't begin to do him justice. He was the one who inspired my pecan pie recipe. I was making a pie one day when he stopped by to visit and spilled some apple moonshine in the pecan goo before it had gone in the oven. It was the best pie I'd ever tasted in my life, and I've never made it any other way."

Great. An old-time love story. That was exactly what he needed right now. “Is there a point to this?”

In a heartbeat, her smile transformed into a glare. “I always have a point to make to those who aren’t too thick-headed to understand it.” She paused, took in a deep breath and clasped her hands together tight enough that her bony knuckles turned white. “One day, not too long after the pie discovery, Josiah’s moonshine still blew up. The explosion took him and everything in the area straight up to Kingdom Come. One moment he was here and then he was gone.” Her voice broke on the last word and she blinked ferociously until the tears threatening to fall surrendered to Ruby Sue’s overwhelming iron will. “I think of him every time I bake a new batch of pies. I remember his smile and his laugh and the way his hand felt on the small of my back when we danced. The memories are a comfort but it doesn’t change the fact that the one man I ever loved is gone, and there’s nothing I can do about it—but *you* can do something about Olivia.”

The ache he’d tried to drink out of existence hit him with full force, battering his ribs and squeezing his chest tight. “She made the right choice to leave.”

“Why, because your face is all scarred up? Do you really think she’s that shallow or are you that dumb?”

That was part of it but there was more. He’d hurt her in the end, and he wouldn’t be able to live with himself. It was better this way. She’d find someone who deserved her. “I’m not someone people should depend on.”

Ruby Sue rolled her eyes. “And yet this whole town does.”

"It's Salvation, the crime rate is pretty much zilch. I'm more figurehead than police chief."

"So your sister and the rest of your family, they don't depend on you?" Exasperation increased her volume and turned her words sharp. "I've seen you with that little munchkin niece of yours. Only a fool would say she couldn't depend on you. Same with others in this town. I know you helped Marna Simons when she broke her hip and needed to get back and forth to physical therapy. Then there's than mangy mutt who thinks you're the best thing since Meaty Bones. All sorts of people depend on you. God knows Olivia depended on you, from the time she was a little one. Your parents were some of the few in town who'd let their kids play with the Sweet triplets. That girl fell in love with you back before she even knew what it meant."

"It's too late." The ache spread through his body until even his bones hurt. "She's gone and if she's smart, she won't come back."

"Then pull your head out of your rump and find a way to get her back to Salvation." Ruby Sue scooted out of the booth and stood at the end of the table staring down at him as if she'd had just about all of his stupid she could take. "Life doesn't give you anything. You have to fight for it. So go fight for that girl."

Without waiting for a response, not that he had any clue what to say, she turned on her heel and marched over to one of the waitresses. Mateo picked up the menu again. He didn't need it, but he needed to do something with his hands because his grasp on what he thought was right was slipping.

It had only ever been sex—amazing sex, the kind of sex that tore him apart and then rebuilt him—but it was just sex. He'd told himself that lie year after year, hotel room after hotel room, pretending that Olivia was just his pre-deployment good-luck charm.

In reality, she was his last wish. If he didn't make it back, he wanted her to be his last good memory, the one that would get him through the darkness and over to the other side.

And he still did.

He may not be the man she deserved, but he could learn to be—he could fight to be.

The waitress stopped at his table, but instead of holding an order pad, she held out a single piece of pecan pie. "Compliments of the house."

Ruby Sue was about as subtle as a Mardi Gras float in the arctic tundra, but she wasn't wrong. He dropped the menu, pulled out his phone and texted his sister.

CHANGE OF PLANS. MEET ME AT THE VETERANS' CENTER.

He had one shot at getting Olivia back—and he needed the whole town's help to make it happen.

Sitting in the middle of the king-size hotel bed, Olivia picked at the remains of the store-bought pecan pie while Handsome shot her death glares from across the room.

"I know you miss swatting at the dog, but we don't belong there." She half-heartedly pushed around the stray pecans in the aluminum pie plate, too tired out from her seventy-two hour crying jag to do more than that. "I don't know where we belong."

Her phone vibrated on the bedside table. Miranda's picture flashed on the screen, not for the first time in the past two days. She didn't want to pick it up. Answering the call meant putting a bright face so no one would know how broken she was.

No. Not broken. Empty, as if someone had taken a giant spoon and scooped out her insides, leaving her nothing more than an aching shell. She'd sold out her family to save the man she loved and he'd shoved her away. How did she explain that to her sisters—to her unborn niece or nephew—when she couldn't explain it to herself? She was an idiot; a flaky idiot with more boobs than brains.

Miranda's photo disappeared off the screen and the vibrations ended. Then it started again, this time with Natalie's picture. If she didn't answer it, they'd have the National Guard searching for her soon. Surrendering to the inevitable, she hit the talk button.

"Oh my God. Where are you?" Natalie asked, worry pushing her voice to a ten on the shrill-o-meter, even with the audible distance added by being on speakerphone.

"I'm at a hotel in Gulch City."

"Are you okay?" Miranda asked.

She glanced up at the mirror on the opposite wall. Her eyes were balloon puffy. Her hair was a greasy mess. She was wearing the same clothes she'd had on when she drove away from Mateo's house. She was most definitely not okay. "I'm fine."

"If you're worried about that asshole Larry, he's not in Salvation anymore. Matteo said he followed him to the county line and that every cop in the county is on the lookout for him just in case he comes back."

Her mutinous heart sped up at the mention of Mateo's name. "When did you talk to him?"

"Yesterday," Natalie said. "He smelled like he'd bathed in a vat of whiskey and looked like he'd been hit by one of the Sweet Salvation Brewery delivery trucks."

"Good." That made her feel better. Misery loved company, even if it was the person who'd ripped out her still-beating heart and put it in a blender.

"You didn't skip town because of Larry," Miranda said.

As always, big sister cut through the bullshit and got right to the heart of it. "No."

"Did something happen with Matteo?" Natalie asked. "We have plenty of eggs in the house and we'll go with you to redecorate his house if you just come home."

Picturing her sister in her signature pastel-colored sweater and with her hair up in a bun, lobbing eggs at Mateo's house, made her lips curl upward for the first time in days. "I appreciate the offer, but I don't think egging the police chief's house is the best plan—even for a Sweet."

"Come home anyway," Miranda said. "We need you back here where you belong."

It's all she'd ever wanted—to belong. She'd grown up in a town where no one ever wanted her and she'd fought back with crazy Sweet attitude. She'd gone into modeling even though people said her curves made her an oddball out, but she'd proved them wrong, landing magazine cover after magazine cover. She'd always had her sisters, but she was the wild child triplet who stuck out.

The only place she'd ever been where she hadn't had to fight to belong was in Mateo's arms. That should have been a huge warning sign that she shouldn't be there. As a Sweet, she knew she had to fight for everything. Anything that came too easy, felt too perfect, was bound to be bad. He'd pushed her away at the hotel. He'd ignored her messages while he was in the VA hospital. He'd told her point blank on his porch to get out of his life.

How many more times did he have to break her heart before she learned that the belonging she felt in his arms was an illusion?

Not another single one.

A hard anger chipped away at the numbness that had settled over her, bringing with it hurt and embarrassment and bitterness.

"I messed up." Again. What was new about her impulsiveness leading to trouble? "When you said you were pregnant, Miranda, I realized the next generation of Sweets couldn't grow up in a town that hated them. But if we could have successfully hosted a fundraiser for the veterans' center, that would have shown the town that the Sweets could bring something good to Salvation. That's why I was so determined to make it a success."

"None of that sounds like a mistake. It sounds amazing," Miranda said.

"It was. Right up until the point when I sold you all out for Mateo." What an idiot she'd been, believing in him—in *them*. "After Mateo got arrested for beating up Larry, the mayor told me he'd make sure the charges didn't stick and that Mateo wouldn't lose his badge. All I had to do was drop my plans for the fundraiser. I didn't know that The Kitchen Sink had surveillance cameras that had captured the whole thing and shown that Larry took the first swing. I thought giving up that chance to bridge the divide between Salvation and the Sweets was the only way to save Mateo."

Family. It's all she'd ever really had and she'd sold it out for a dream that wasn't ever going to be a reality. The realization ripped through her like claws through butter.

"Like an idiot, I loved him. I sold out my family for a man who had never loved me and never would."

"You didn't sell us out," Miranda sniffled. "You made the right choice, and one all of us support."

"Fuck him," Natalie said. "Fuck them both."

The shock of Natalie's words slapped Olivia out of her personal pity party. "What did you say?"

"You heard me," Natalie said, her words flowing with NASCAR speed. "Your idea for the fundraiser is a great one. We're not going to let Tyrell Hawson blackmail us into not doing it. If he wants to shut down one of us Sweets, he'll have to shut down *all* of us, and good luck to him if the fool tries that." She sucked in a quick breath. "As for Mateo, if he can't see what an amazing woman you are, then he is the dumbest asshole on the face of the earth and we don't have time for that kind of foolishness. It's just not efficient."

The sound of Natalie flipping through papers on her ever-present clipboard came over the phone line. "Okay, the fundraiser is scheduled for Saturday, so we have two days to finalize all the details and get everything in place. You've already put together a plan of attack, I'm a whiz at organizing everything to get it in place, and I feel sorry for anyone who gets in Miranda's way when she's negotiating with the other breweries so they get their kegs here on time for the competitive beer tasting." She smacked the clipboard down on something hard. "Everyone in Salvation is about to learn that when you take on one of the Sweets, you take on us all. Hurry up and get your ass in the car and come home, Olivia, we have a fundraiser to put on."

The phone went dead. All she could do was stare at it as she tried to process what in the hell had just happened.

"Mrow," the cat called from her perch on the windowsill.

"Exactly." She got up and tossed the bland pecan pie into the trashcan, a lightness to her steps that hadn't been there for days.

Her heart was battered, her self-confidence shaken and she had no idea if they could pull off the fundraiser, but it didn't matter. She was going home to Salvation. It was where she belonged.

Chapter Thirteen

Shirtsleeves still damp from the dog splashing water on him during his bath this morning, Mateo walked into the Salvation County Courthouse. It was quiet on a Saturday morning, with most everyone off duty. The dog's freshly trimmed nails click-clacked on the marble floor as they crossed the lobby to the mayor's office.

Peeking into the other county and city offices as he passed, he spotted Sweet Salvation Brewery growlers on countertops, along with placards explaining that the change collected would go toward building a new veterans' center. He'd dropped them off yesterday morning and they were already more than halfway full.

All anyone had been talking about for the past few days was the veterans' center fundraiser. Olivia had called in God knew how many favors and people were flying in from all over to help raise money. Every woman he knew had bought a handful of raffle tickets to win a makeover by some famous stylist who had his own TV show. Salvation had been talking about the Sweets for generations and Olivia had figured out how to use it as an advantage. No doubt about it, there was a helluva lot more to the woman than just her looks.

Not that he'd seen her since she came back from wherever she'd been holed up. He had to get his troops positioned correctly first. No Marine went into battle without a plan. And now it was time to pull out the big guns.

He pushed open the mayor's office door.

Hawson sat behind his desk with a scowl on his face. "What do you want?"

So they were bypassing the pleasantries. This was Mateo's kind of conversation. "You're going to the veterans' center fundraiser at the Sweet Salvation Brewery today."

"I most certainly am not."

Oh he was; he just didn't know it yet. Having the mayor show up would prove to Salvation's last anti-Sweet holdouts that the family couldn't be vilified anymore. It's what Olivia wanted and what he was determined to deliver.

Mateo stepped around the desk and Hawson flinched. The fear in the other man's eyes was well founded, but that wasn't the kind of damage he planned on inflicting if the mayor didn't follow orders like a good Marine.

"I'm telling you right now, you're going to go." Mateo kept his tone light, but there was no way the other man could miss the underlying threat. "Not only that, but you are going to act like there is nowhere you'd rather be than at that fundraiser."

"Why would I do that?" he sputtered.

Now to hit the power-hungry mayor exactly where it hurt. "Because there's an election coming up—and if you don't act like the Sweets are one of the most important families in Salvation, *I'll* run for mayor."

Hawson blanched.

"You've pissed off a lot of people over the years, but have always managed to keep anyone from running against you." Mateo sat down on Hawson's desk, scattering papers and knocking over a cup full of pens. "How do you like your odds against a Marine injured in the line of duty who rescues dogs from kill shelters and beats up blackmailers?"

"You're not a people-person." The other man's voice went up an octave. "There's absolutely no glad-handing politician in you. You'd hate everything about running for office and keeping it."

"True." It would be a living fucking hell. "But I'd still do it—and I'd win. We both know it."

Hawson fidgeted with a pen and a red flush crept up his neck. "I don't believe you."

Mateo got up, sending a stack of papers sailing down to the floor. "That's your prerogative, but you'll find out the truth if you don't show up for that fundraiser. It's about to start and you don't want to be late."

Neither did he. The first bus to the brewery left from The Kitchen Sink's parking lot in ten minutes. Without a second look at the mayor, he crossed the room to where the dog waited by the door.

"I see hanging out with Olivia Sweet has had quite the effect on you," the mayor called out.

Mateo looked back. "You're right. It has."

Now to go convince Olivia of that.

Every table in front of the Sweet Salvation Brewery was packed with people. The five lines for the beer tasting were ten-people deep. Olivia had already emptied out the collection growlers at the tables twice. The live band had kept the dance floor grooving since its first set. Half in awe, she stood with her sisters and surveyed the crowd.

"Can you believe it?" she asked Miranda.

"Of course I can." Her sister grinned. "No one can stop the wild Sweet once she sets her mind to something."

The band stopped in the middle of a song and feedback sounded from the speakers, making everyone wince.

"Sorry about that, folks," the mayor said.

Olivia's stomach sank. There was no way this was going to go well, but short of tackling Tyrell Hawson and tearing the mic from his grasp, there wasn't much she could do but weather this latest storm.

"I'd like to thank the Sweet Salvation Brewery and the Sweet family for hosting such an amazing event for such an important cause to our community," he said. Then he raised a mug of beer. "I hope you'll join me in raising a toast to Miranda, Natalie and Olivia Sweet for all they're doing to make Salvation a better community." Everyone clapped and the mayor took a healthy swig of beer. "Now don't forget why we're all here today. Be sure to enter the raffles and participate in the beer tasting. All of the proceeds will go to building a new veterans' center."

Everyone cheered.

"Do you think he's drunk?" Miranda asked.

Dumbfounded, Olivia shook her head. "He didn't slur."

"Here comes another bus," Natalie said as she handed Olivia a roll of raffle tickets. "Go get 'em."

Still trying to work out the mayor's change of heart, she made her way to the edge of the open-air beer garden to greet the newcomers. After handing out raffle tickets to what seemed like half the town, she realized the bus was still in the parking lot. The driver should have shut the doors and gone back for another group by now, but it remained parked with the doors open.

Figuring there was someone on board who needed assistance getting off, she began walking over, but Mateo's dog appeared in the doorway.

He paused for a second, happily panting as he looked around. The moment he spotted Olivia, he turned into a multicolored fur flash as he sprinted down the steps and across the parking lot to her.

"What in the world are you doing here?" She knelt down to pet him, keeping her eye on the bus, figuring Luciana and her brood were about to debark, but no one did. Looking down at the dog, she noticed he had a brand new bright-yellow collar. A rolled-up piece of paper dangled from it.

Heart fluttering, she glanced up, looking for Mateo. He was the only who would send his dog with a note, but he wasn't mingling in the crowd. Fingers shaking, she unhooked the note from the dog's collar while dodging the happy guy's licks as much as possible.

HI, MY NAME'S TROUBLE. MY PERSON IS AN IDIOT. CAN YOU HELP ME FIND HIM?

She bit her bottom lip to stop the quivering and buried her face in Trouble's soft fur. Her heart was held together with weak glue and Scotch tape; another swift kick by Mateo's boot and she wasn't sure she'd be able to put it back together again.

Even though it was the last thing she should do, she looked up at the bus. The doors were still open. He had to be in there. Excitement, hope and a belief in happily ever afters pushed its way to the forefront. It lightened her footsteps as she walked toward the bus, the dog following behind.

But before she reached it, the driver closed the doors and the bus rolled forward on its return trip to Salvation.

One by one, the butterflies fluttering in her stomach dropped dead as the bus pulled away. It wasn't until it was almost out of the lot that she could see who had been hiding behind it.

Mateo stood alone in the parking lot wearing a T-shirt that read: I'M THE IDIOT.

Mateo watched four thousand expressions flitter across Olivia's face, but she didn't move. Okay, he was prepared for this. Mostly. Walking over to her with the caution of a man picking up a live grenade, he mentally prepared for the worst while hoping like hell things wouldn't go FUBAR double quick.

"You've got a lot of nerve." She crossed her arms and glared at him.

"I have to." He got close enough to smell her strawberry body wash and feel the heat of her anger. Even with that, though, the electricity sparking between them could have lit up a Third World country. "You'd eat a less stubborn man for breakfast."

Her lips twitched upward, but she recovered fast and returned to resting bitch face. "Am I supposed to find that charming?"

"I've never been accused of having a lot of charm. I'm pigheaded, grouchy and I say the wrong things at the worst time. Basically, I'm an asshole—but I'm *your* asshole." *Fuck. Brain, anytime you want to catch up with the mouth, that would be good.* "That didn't come out right. Hell, I don't know what to say." He shoved his hand through his hair, sucked in a deep breath and tried again. "All I know is that when I'm around you, everything is better. When I'm not around you, I'm like a wounded animal snarling at anyone who dares to come near. You're beautiful and smart and you don't put up with any of my shit. We work together. We always have."

He paused, trying to judge by the look on her face if he was making any sense at all because to his own ears, he sounded totally unhinged. Olivia's chin trembled and her nose had turned red. Her eyes were watery. He really *was* an idiot. He was fucking this all up, but he couldn't stop talking.

"I guess what I'm trying to say is that we belong together." The words rushed out. "I love you, Olivia Sweet. I'm not the man you deserve, but I hope someday I will be."

"You idiot." Olivia stopped his rambling. "You already are."

He pulled her close before she could change her mind and kissed her as Trouble howled his approval.

Chapter Fourteen

Six Months Later

The cabin's living room was littered with women's clothing, makeup brushes, hair tools and chocolate wrappers.

"This is so Sweet of us," Olivia giggled, excited jitters bubbling up inside her even as she knew there was no place else she'd rather be than here where she belonged—and no one that she'd rather be with today, tomorrow and forever.

Miranda shook her head as she rubbed her two-weeks-to-go belly. "Ruby Sue said she expected it of us."

"Really, it's the most streamlined way to do this," Natalie said, and tucked an errant hair behind her ear.

Olivia looked at her sisters, both dressed in head-to-toe white, just like she was. Miranda, with her swollen belly, was in a white-cotton sundress and a simple lace veil. Natalie wore a white sheath dress topped with a lightweight cotton sweater with pearl buttons traveling up the middle. For herself, it was a simple white-silk maxi dress and flowers in her hair. The whole thing was completely crazy and made perfect sense at the same time.

"Salvation won't forget about this wedding for a while," Natalie said as she turned to face them.

"Yep." Miranda waddled forward. "The guys can't say they went into this thinking they were marrying into a normal family."

Olivia gave her sisters a quick squeeze. "Okay, let's do this."

She pushed open the cabin's front door and walked out into the field surrounded by trees whose leaves were at the peak of their fall red, gold and orange beauty, despite the unexpected warm weather so late in the season. The sun warmed her face as her gaze automatically sought out Mateo. He stood near a freshly painted arbor flanked by Logan and Sean. Her heart sped up at the sight of him, just like it always had. Just like it always would. The wedding march started and she stepped forward toward Mateo and her future.

Most of the town had come to watch the proceedings. Ruby Sue had her seat in the front row. Luciana and her family took up most of the second. No one in Salvation wanted to miss a Sweet triple wedding.

The ceremony flew by in a flash and before she knew it, she was wearing a simple gold band on her finger and facing Mateo.

"I now pronounce you husbands and wives," the minister said. "Gentlemen, you may kiss your brides."

Mateo dipped his head lower and his lips brushed across hers. Soft. Sexy. Promising more later, after all the people vacated his property and it was just them. It was everything Olivia always wanted and more. So much more.

"Oh my God!" Miranda squealed. "My water just broke."

Chaos erupted.

Half the people in attendance whipped out their cell phones to call 911 or take photos to better document for later gossip sessions at The Kitchen Sink—it *was* Salvation, after all—and the rest surged forward to crowd around Miranda. Logan swept up his new bride, cradling her in his arms, and took off running toward his truck parked in Mateo's drive. They drove away down the driveway, the "just married" streamers tied to his antenna flying in the wind and the cans tied to his bumper clanging against the ground.

"Hope you weren't expecting things to get back to normal in your life, now that you've married into the Sweet family," Olivia said.

Mateo threw back his head and laughed. "I think trouble is my new normal, and I wouldn't have it any other way—as long as I have you."

"You'll always have me." Rising up on her tiptoes, she brushed her lips across his. "Now let's go before we miss everything."

Olivia grabbed Mateo's hand and they joined everyone else rushing to their cars to get to the hospital for the birth of the first in the next generation of Sweets.

A Note From Avery

Hey you!

I really hope you enjoyed Olivia and Mateo—plus Handsome and Trouble, too. They were a blast to write. If you have a second to leave a review of Trouble on Tap, that would be awesome.

Please stay in touch (avery@averyflynn.com), I love hearing from readers. Want to get all the latest book news? Subscribe to my newsletter for book gossip, monthly prizes and more.

Don't forget to check out my other Sweet Salvation Brewery books: Enemies on Tap and Hollywood on Tap. Keep reading for an excerpt of both!

xoxo,

Avery

Books By Avery Flynn

The Killer Style Series

High-Heeled Wonder (Killer Style 1)
This Year's Black (Killer Style 2)
Make Me Up (Killer Style 3)

Sweet Salvation Brewery Series

Enemies on Tap (Sweet Salvation Brewery 1)
Hollywood on Tap (Sweet Salvation Brewery 2)
Trouble on Tap (Sweet Salvation Brewery 3)

Dangerous Love Series

Dangerous Kiss (Laytons 1)
Dangerous Flirt (Laytons 2)
Dangerous Tease (Laytons 3)

Novellas

Hot Dare (Dare to Love Kindle World)
Daring Ink (Dare to Love Kindle World)
Betting the Billionaire
Jax and the Beanstalk Zombies (Fairy True 1)
Big Bad Red (Fairy True 2)

Newsletter

Subscribe to Avery's newsletter for news about her latest releases, giveaways and more!

Street Team

Join the Flynnbots and get sneak peeks at Avery's latest books and more!

Visit Avery's website at www.averyflynn.com

Facebook: https://www.facebook.com/AveryFlynnAuthor

TSU: https://www.tsu.co/AveryFlynn

Pinterest: https://www.pinterest.com/averyflynnbooks/

Twitter: https://twitter.com/averyflynn

E-mail: avery@averyflynn.com

Enemies on Tap

(Sweet Salvation Brewery 1) Excerpt

"Tell me something, Miranda." Giving into the need ready to eat him alive, Logan positioned himself between her open legs and placed his palms flat on either side of her luscious hips.

The pulse in her neck kept pace with his own rapid heart rate, and his body throbbed with want. He couldn't help but inhale a deep breath of her teasing scent. If he didn't watch it, he'd be falling for the enemy. Again.

"What counts as fair?"

Her teeth raked across her bottom lip before she sucked it in. "Stop bribing contractors not to work with me."

He shouldn't just say no, but hell no. That squirrelly guy from the brewery had been right. Logan hated to lose. Hated. It. But he didn't give a rat's ass about all of that right now, not with Miranda so close he could count each one of the freckles decorating her cleavage until they disappeared beneath the V of her sweater. Even with the bet and their personal history hanging over them, he needed to count the freckles hidden by the soft cashmere.

Could there be a way if they fought fair? Was he ready to take that bet?

Miranda's tongue swiped across the center of her very pink bottom lip, but her hooded gaze never wavered from his eyes.

Logan slid his hands over her jeans until his palms lay across her firm thighs, thumbs against the raised inseam of her jeans. The feel of her against him heightened everything except his sense of self-preservation. Fuck it. He was all in.

"I'll stop bribing contractors not to work with you."

The single sentence hung in the inch of air between them. Tension pulled his balls tight, and need swirled at the base of his spine. Primal. Bone deep. All-encompassing. Worlds were created or destroyed in moments like this.

She flexed her muscles beneath his touch, leaning forward as her lips parted. "I don't want to want you, and this doesn't change anything." Her words brushed against his parted lips, taunting him with their nearness. "I still hate your guts."

"Liar." His mouth crashed down to hers, and he surrendered to the combustible cocktail of frustration, lust, and something too new to define drowning them both.

Hollywood on Tap

(Sweet Salvation Brewery 2) Excerpt

The walk–in cooler stood twenty feet away.

So frickin' close that Sean O'Dell could practically smell the flowery green hops and feel them crumble in his palms.

The weight on his chest eased with each step. He was going to close out the day without having yet another conversation with Natalie about lean manufacturing or whatever the hell system the

people at Toyota invented. She'd been hounding him all day to sit down with her and go over her crazy–ass plans to streamline the brewery process. As if the craft and creativity of making beer could be distilled down to numbers on a spreadsheet. The woman was as annoyingly persistent as she was hot—both were a distraction he didn't need in his life right now, not with the Southeast Brewers Invitational coming up.

But for the next thirteen hours, he wouldn't have to hear any of her harebrained recommendations. He reached for the cooler's door handle and turned it, noticing as he did so that it wasn't latched.

He yanked open the door before his brain processed the ants dancing up his spine.

The motion triggered the cooler's sensor activated overhead lights. His gut dipped and he clenched his jaw.

Natalie stood shivering on the other side of the cooler's threshold, clutching her damn clipboard to her chest.

He stopped cold. "What in the hell are you doing here?"

"Waiting for you in your favorite hiding spot." Her teeth chattered. "Do you really think I don't know your secrets?"

God knew exactly how long she'd been lying in wait for him, but it was enough time for her button nose to turn red and her glasses to frost over. His gaze slid to the right. The temperature gage read twenty–six.

A smarter man would have shut the door and walked away, let her deal with the consequences of spending time in the Sweet Salvation Brewery's cooler without a coat. But no one—from his asshole of a father to his always–hungry–for–more agent to his on–set teachers—had ever accused him of having an overabundance of brains.

Instead, he whipped off his thick hoodie and pulled it over her head. Not bothering to get her arms through the sleeves, he wrapped her up—clipboard and all—inside its fleece warmth. The hood drooped over her head, covering everything down to her nose. Before she could squeak out a noise over the chattering of her teeth, he wrapped an arm around her narrow waist and tossed her over one shoulder like a sack of grain. Her cold seeped into him, pouring over his body and making him shiver.

"P–p–put me down." She made a halfhearted attempt to wriggle free.

"No." He spun around and kicked the cooler door shut with his boot heel.

"This is unseemly."

Her body may be half a degree away from being a snow cone, but holding her like this had him running a few degrees warmer. "Yep."

"You can't just carry me around like this," Natalie huffed against his lower back. "I'm your boss."

"I can and you are." But he was bound to forget that last part if she kept squirming against him. Hell, he couldn't seem to remember that fact while he was alone at night staring at his bedroom ceiling and imagining how those damn little buttons would open under his touch.

Made in the USA
San Bernardino, CA
18 July 2019